A Season of Dreams

Sharon Westra

PublishAmerica
Baltimore

© 2003 by Sharon Westra.
All rights reserved. No part of this book may be reproduced in any form without written permission from the publishers, except by a reviewer who may quote brief passages in a review to be printed in a newspaper or magazine.

First printing

ISBN: 1-59286-843-6
PUBLISHED BY PUBLISHAMERICA BOOK PUBLISHERS
www.publishamerica.com
Baltimore

Printed in the United States of America

Dedicated to:

Elaine Nibler, who was there at the beginning…
and
The teenage girl students—past, present, and future—at Mount Vernon Christian School, who visit the school library and share their passion for books with me.

~To God be the glory~
who nurtured the dream all these years
and brought it to fruition.

The most heartfelt thank you to:

My loving husband, Paul, who believed in me, supported me and encouraged me. Without you, I never would have taken even the first step. You offered invaluable advice, kept me true to myself, and gave up your time to help me with all those computer related details.

My friend, Judy Adeline, who loves this book almost as if it were her own. She spent countless hours reading, editing, questioning, and making suggestions. Judy, thank you for the season you spent living this story with me. I could not have done it without you.

Rick Bury and Brad Vos who helped with some details.

All others who offered help and support in any way.

The people at Publish America, who were willing to give this book a chance.

Scripture quotations taken from the HOLY BIBLE, NEW INTERNATIONAL VERSION. Copyright 1973, 1978, 1984 by International Bible Society. Used by permission of Zondervan Publishing House.

PROLOGUE

September rain pelted against the dormitory window and raced in rivulets down the glass. Gray skies matched Katie's melancholy mood as she paged restlessly through a nursing journal. Sighing, she shoved it aside and leaned back against the chair. She could not concentrate on her studies today. Perhaps it was the weather. It was the first dark and dreary day of autumn. Katie knew that this was just the first of many dark days that would be coming with winter. She closed her eyes and prayed for strength. Slowly pulling open her desk drawer, she withdrew three photographs. She gazed fondly at the top one, a 3x5 studio print of a girl about her own age. The girl was pretty with short brunette hair and a few freckles on her straight nose. Her face was animated with a perky smile and laughing brown eyes. Written in a flourish across the corner of the picture was 'Forever, Diana.'

Katie smiled and her heart warmed a little as she laid the picture on the top of her open textbook and then turned to the next photo. It was a wallet-sized print of a boy in his late teens. He had a copper colored suntan, unruly brown hair, mischievous eyes and a playful grin. This picture was simply signed 'Wayne.' Katie's smile faded as her eyes were drawn to the last photograph. It was a 5x7 print portraying a handsome young man. She lingered over this picture, taking in every detail. The boy's hair was light blond, his eyes a bright cornflower blue. He had a ruddy complexion, a sincere smile.

"If only…" the words were barely above a whisper as Katie sighed again. A shiver ran through her and she turned misty-eyed to the window, but her reverie was suddenly interrupted as Sara, her roommate, bounced into the room.

"You've got mail!" Sara announced, waving an envelope in the air for Katie to see.

"Good," Katie said, forcing a cheerfulness she did not feel into her voice. "Who's it from?"

"I don't know," Sara replied, holding the envelope up. "There's no return address. It just says 'Anderson.'" Handing the letter to Katie, she queried, "Anderson, who?"

Katie's heart skipped a beat as she took the envelope with trembling fingers. She looked at it carefully to read the postmark. Montana. Her green eyes moved to the name written in the top left corner of the envelope. Anderson. She closed her eyes and pressed the envelope between her palms. Hope surged through her as she contemplated what news the letter might contain.

"Well," Sara persisted, "is it a she Anderson or a he Anderson? I can tell from the look on your face that it's somebody special."

"It's …umm…just an old friend."

"Katie, I can tell that you would like some privacy. I'll go down and get us each a mocha and bagel from the coffee shop. Maybe when I get back, you'll want to fill me in on some details. I'm beginning to think there is a lot more to Miss Katie Fremont than meets the eye." Sara reached for her purse, gave Katie a pat on the shoulder and headed out.

Katie sat in a daze until the door was firmly closed behind her friend, and then, with fingers that nearly fumbled from anticipation, she tore open the envelope. Pulling out a single sheet of yellow paper, the kind from a legal pad, she began to read the hand-written letter.

Dear Katie,

Ever since Valentine's Day, I haven't been able to stop thinking about you, especially since I left. I hope and pray that you are okay and settling into dorm life at college. I'm sorry that I didn't write sooner, but as I told you last spring, I wasn't ready. You were probably right when you said we should be comforting each other, but it was something that I had to work out by myself.

Actually, I'm sorry for a lot of things. Things I did and didn't do. Things I did and didn't say. I know that you were on the receiving end of most of those things. Now I feel that I am ready to talk about it all; to share with someone...well, not just anyone, but with you. So many things need to be settled between us. Things that need to be put right.

My heart aches. I'm wondering if yours does too...

Katie looked up from the letter and dropped it onto her lap as tears trickled down her cheeks. Reaching for the photographs, she clasped them in her hands and hugged them to her heart. She could remember it all. Every detail: the colors, the sounds, the smells...she could still see it, still hear it, still feel it. She just had to close her eyes to relive it.

Part I

Chapter 1

FIRST SIGHT

Katie sighed as she put the last CD into the rack on her desk. *That just about does it*, she thought as she glanced around her room. It was painted pale yellow and her blue floral comforter was on the bed. White curtains fluttered in the evening breeze. Scenic posters and photographs of friends plastered the walls. Hearing a light tap on her bedroom door, Katie turned as it opened, and her cousin, Diana, stuck her brunette head into the room.

"It's looking good, Kate!" Diana's glance took in the cheery room with the posters and knick-knacks put in place. "I still find it hard to believe you actually live here now. We are going to have so much fun this last year of high school!"

"You and Nikki are the only bright spots in this move of Dad's," Katie's response referred to Diana's younger sister. Her serious reply did not match her cousin's upbeat welcome. "If it weren't for the two of you I don't know what I'd do."

"I'm sure it's very tough having to move right before your senior year and I know I'd want to curl up and die if I was in your place, but I am *so* happy you're here! It's a great chance for us to live close by and go to school together. I plan to do everything that I can to make the adjustment easier for you – that's why I'm here. I'm meeting some friends at the Dairy Shack and I want you to come along so I can introduce you."

Although Diana and Katie had always lived far apart, they had managed to keep a close relationship thriving. They had enough in common to share thoughts and have good times, but they were enough different to keep things interesting. Their families participated in family reunions about every three years. In between reunions, the girls had been able to maintain their closeness by visiting occasionally and sending frequent letters and emails across the nation.

Katie had dreaded this move to Washington State. She loved her cousin, and considered Diana her best friend, but it was, after all, senior year. It took time and energy to make new friends and establish a reputation. She knew she could be miserable, or trust God and rely on Diana and…

Katie nodded her head, "That's a good idea. I *will* come with you." She slipped on a pair of sandals and grabbed her purse. After checking with Katie's mom, the two girls took off in Diana's dark blue car. Within thirty minutes, they were seated at a round table enjoying ice cream sundaes with three of Diana's friends. Jessica was well into a humorous story about her day care job when four teen-aged boys sauntered in the door and up to the counter. Katie's gaze was drawn to the foursome, but rested on the blond who had entered the restaurant last.

"Who's he?" she whispered to Diana, indicating the handsome, fair-haired young man who stood a little behind the other three at the counter. "Does he go to our school?"

"Which one?" Diana turned to look. " Oh," she said, following Katie's gaze, "that's Steve Anderson."

"Isn't he a dream?" Tami sighed.

Lisa leaned in closer to the girls around the table and quietly added, "He's such a catch. Half the girls in school have a crush on him."

"So, tell me about him," Katie urged. She studied the boy who had become the topic of discussion around the table. He stood nearly six feet tall. His hair was short and very blond, and even from this distance, Katie could tell that he had piercing blue eyes.

"He's absolutely the cutest guy in our class," Tami said. "He's one of those kind of guys that seems to have everything going for him: good grades, a nice personality, and he's a natural athlete. He's an awesome soccer player. He's the goalie on our school team."

"He's really good," Jessica put in. "He was on varsity as a sophomore. And the best thing is that he's humble about it, too."

"He is very nice. Really sweet and thoughtful," Diana added.

"Does he have a girlfriend?" Katie wanted to know. "He must."

"No, and I don't know why not," Tami replied. "He could have any girl he wanted. He's taken a couple out to school events, but nothing serious. Lisa wasn't kidding. Most of the girls in school would love to date him."

Katie turned her full attention to Diana, looking directly into her cousin's brown eyes. "Do you want to date him? Are you wishing he would ask you out?"

"Me?" Diana laughed. "Not in a million years! Steve's a really neat guy, but not my type. I want someone who takes life a little less seriously. Take his friend, Wayne, over there." Diana nodded toward the dark-haired, dark-eyed youth walking toward the pool table with a milkshake in his hand. "Tall, dark, handsome, funny, musical; what more could a girl want?"

The girls' talk turned to other things as Diana and her friends acquainted Katie with school news. They spoke of teachers and classes and the extra-curricular activities offered at their small Christian high school. An hour or so later, deciding it was time to leave, Tami, Jessica and Lisa rose from the table. Diana exchanged goodbyes with her friends, but remained seated. Waiting until the other three girls had left the restaurant, she turned to Katie and said, "I didn't want to say anything in front of the others, but Steve has had his eye on you the entire time that he's been playing pool."

"Not really!" Katie said, feeling flustered.

"I'm not kidding, Katie. I think he is very interested in what he sees."

The idea that he had been watching her, was perhaps even interested in meeting her, thrilled Katie. She did not have very much experience dating boys, but this one looked special. Finding it hard to believe that someone so cute would find her interesting, she offered an idea to Diana, "Maybe he's been watching you."

Diana laughed. "I doubt that, cousin of mine! I've gone to school with the guy since the sixth grade. Shhh, be quiet," she added, under her breath. "Wayne is coming over."

Katie casually turned to watch the person that Diana had referred to as Wayne approach their table. He was taller than the blond was, reaching a few inches over six feet. He had broad shoulders and his thick, brown hair was somewhat messy. When he reached the table, he leaned on it nonchalantly. "So, Di, who's your new friend?"

Diana's eyes twinkled and she answered saucily, "Who wants to know? You or a certain blond friend of yours?"

"Well," Wayne shrugged and nodded toward his three buddies. "We've all been wondering. You know, a new girl in town is cause for attention."

Katie felt herself blushing, but Diana just giggled. "If you must know, she's my cousin, Katie Fremont. Her family just moved to town. Her dad is the new pastor at my church." Diana turned to Katie. "Katie, meet Wayne Anderson."

Katie gave Diana a confused look and said uncertainly, "But I thought you said his friend's name was Anderson."

Wayne laughed. "Ah-ha! Caught you!" he teased, his brown eyes shining. "Looks like we guys aren't the only curious ones around here. Do you want to explain, Diane, or should I? We mustn't leave your cousin in the dark."

"It's like this, Katie," Diana began to explain, "Steve and Wayne are adopted brothers, but also best friends. When the boys were little, Steve and Wayne's parents were very good friends and guardians of each other's kids. Wayne was an only child and when he was eight years old, his parents were killed in a car accident. Steve's parents adopted him. Now they share a family and a last name, but they're also best friends."

"That is a sad story," Katie responded sympathetically. "But there is also something very touching about it. It almost makes me want to cry."

Wayne looked across the room to where Steve stood, watching, holding his pool cue in his hands. "She's a keeper," Wayne announced loud enough for most of the customers to hear.

Steve grinned, dimples flashing, but Katie buried her face in her hands in embarrassment. Diana clapped her hands together and exclaimed, "Hmmm....why do I think this is the beginning of something special?"

Chapter 2

SOMETHING SPECIAL

The next morning, Steve and Wayne sat alone at the breakfast table, as their mother had a breakfast meeting for a school project and their dad had already left for work. Their two younger brothers had taken large bowls of cereal into the family room so they would not miss any of their favorite morning cartoons.

"So, are you going to ask her out, Bro?" Wayne asked as he buttered his toast.

"I'm not sure yet."

"You're not sure yet? Steve, why do you always analyze everything to death?"

"You know I've never felt I had time for a girlfriend. She'd have to be something really special for me to make a move like that."

Wayne looked his brother in the eye. "I think she is some kind of special. I think you're going to find that out. And if you don't move soon, once school starts some other guy is going to find it out and poof!" Wayne snapped his fingers. "She'll be gone."

"But why would she want to go out with *me*? I never even talked to her." Steve set down his glass of orange juice, looked at his brother and continued, "If I could get to know her just a little before I asked her out, you know, so I could be sure I want to get started with something..."

"How about if the four of us go out? You and me and Katie and Diane. We'll go as a group, but we'll all know that it's really about you and her."

"Oh, yeah? How would *we* all know that unless you say something to the girls?" Steve challenged Wayne, raising his eyebrows in question.

"Because of last night at the Shack. The electricity going back and forth between the two of you was so strong I'm surprised your hair wasn't standing on end. You couldn't take your eyes off her, and believe me, she was interested in you, too!"

"Okay, you're right, I admit it, I am interested in her. Let's do it. Let's go for pizza, but let's meet them at the restaurant so if nothing comes of it there won't be any awkward goodnights when it's time to go home."

"And if something does come from it?" Wayne waved his toast in front of Steve's face.

"Then, my man, you'll have to walk home."

Diana, dressed in overall-jean shorts, a red shirt, and tennis shoes, entered Katie's bedroom. Her brown hair was cut short around her face and she sported wispy bangs; a few freckles were sprinkled across her nose.

"Hi," she greeted her cousin. "Your mom said you were getting ready and I could come on up." Diana took in the different clothing items spread about on Katie's bed. "Can't decide what to wear, huh?"

Katie turned from the mirror above her dresser. She was putting clips in her hair, to keep the long blond strands out of her face. She was not very tall, standing only about five feet, five inches. Her eyes were green and her complexion was fair. She was dressed in a casual sundress with Hawaiian flowers in the print. "I had decided on this, but I'm not really sure. You're wearing shorts. This is probably too dressy."

"It's perfect. It's very you, Katie. Pretty, feminine, romantic. You know I never wear dresses, except on Sundays. Grab a sweater though, because the nights around here tend to get very cool, even in August."

"Okay, if you think it's fine." Katie opened a drawer and drew out a pale yellow cardigan sweater.

"Trust me," Diana assured her. "I've never steered you wrong before, have I?"

"Hmmm...let me think," Katie put a finger to her forehead in mock contemplation. "I happen to remember a time we were camping in Oregon. We had been playing on a playground and when we wanted to go back to camp, we had an argument about which trail to take. It seems to me, we followed your suggestion and ended up lost and crying at the ranger's station."

Diana smiled at the memory. "Give me a break, we were only nine years old."

"Then there was that time in eighth grade when you flew out to visit during spring vacation. You convinced me we should practice driving my dad's car in the church parking lot. I'm quite sure your last words to me were 'Trust me' right before you accidentally put the car in reverse instead of drive and plowed into that light pole."

Diana chuckled. "Okay, okay, but I've gained much discernment since I started high school."

"I don't know," Katie slipped out of her dress. "I think I'll wear shorts like you." She pulled on a pair of white jean shorts, a navy blue shirt and her sandals. Picking up her sweater from the bed she said, "Okay, I'm ready now. Let's go."

Diana pulled her blue car into a parking spot in front of the Pizza Ranch. "I hope they're here already. I hate waiting for a date."

"This is not a date, Di," Katie said as she brushed her long blond hair over her shoulder. "It's just a get-together for pizza. You know, 'Let's be nice to the new girl.'"

Diana stared at her cousin. "Maybe that's the way they do things where you come from, Miss Naivety, but around here, this is a date. This is a casual, let's-get-to-know-her date."

"What about you, then? You'll be here with the man of your dreams. You know, the 'tall, dark, handsome, funny' one."

Diana opened the car door. "Don't kid yourself or tease me, Katie. Wayne and I are here as security. Nothing more."

"How do you *know* these things?" Katie grabbed her sweater off the seat before shutting her car door.

"Trust me, Kate. I've learned a thing or two since I was little. But you're right. Even if I am here as Steve's security blanket, my companion will be tall and dashing. Come on." With that, Diana led the way into the dimly lit restaurant. Spotting the guys at a booth in the corner, she put her arm through Katie's and propelled them both toward the red-checkered table.

"Wayne, they're here." Steve had been watching the door. He half stood, encumbered by the bench being too close to the table, and greeted Katie. "Hi. I'm Steve. I guess we were never actually introduced last night." He directed all his attention to Katie, staring into her green eyes.

"I'm Katie," she answered shyly.

"Why don't you sit here," Steve indicated the space on the bench next to him. Katie slid into the booth, and while Steve's gaze lingered on her, she grinned at Diana and Wayne.

"Steve," Wayne cleared his throat. "Look who else is here. Why, it's Diane!"

"That's okay," Diana whispered in his ear. "I know why you and I are here. Security blankets."

Wayne laughed, a deep hearty laugh and his brown eyes sparkled. Steve blushed and half rose again. "Sorry, Di. Glad you could come."

They settled into their booth, ordered pizza and poured themselves sodas.

"So, where are you from?" Steve turned to Katie. "I hear you just moved to town."

"The southern part of Minnesota. My dad was pastor there for seven years. Before that, we lived in Michigan, where I was born."

"Lucky you," Wayne said. "You've been around. Seen some of the country." Katie smiled. "I'd hardly call a little bit of the Midwest 'seeing the country'. I've never really been anywhere except for coming out here."

"Except for my uncle's in San Francisco, I've never been many places either," Wayne confided. "I bet you must have seen something neat on your trip out here. Tell us what the most interesting thing was."

Katie shrugged. "I don't know. My dad was really pushing to get here. We had the big moving van so we didn't go to Mount Rushmore or Yellowstone or any of the tourist sites along the way."

"Well, there must have been something special that you saw." Wayne persisted, "Think about it, I really want to know."

Steve had an understanding grin on his face, as he watched this conversation take place between his brother, who yearned to travel, and, dare he think, his date? Katie seemed to be everything he had hoped she would be. Pretty, soft-spoken, polite. He could not wait to get to know her better.

Katie had leaned her head back and closed her eyes for a moment. Opening them, she said, "Do you know that in late summer, from one end of Montana to the other, and I'm talking about hundreds and hundreds of miles from the east side to the west side, wild Black-eyed Susans grow along the highway? It's beautiful."

"That's cool," Wayne nodded his head. "I never knew that. Someday, when I'm traveling across the country, which I am going to do, I'll think of you when I see those Black Susans or whatever they're called. I've got goals for traveling someday and I'm going to see America. I want to go to other countries, too."

"Tell them about the trip, Wayne," Steve encouraged.

"My uncle Brad is a bachelor and pretty well off. I guess he deals in real estate and has a lot of investments. He's traveled all over the world so maybe I inherited his sense of adventure. Anyway, he wants to take Steve and me to South America. He promised to pay half of our expenses. We're planning to go in two summers. At first it was going to be a graduation trip this coming summer, but Steve and I need some time to earn enough money."

"I am sure you'll have a fabulous time." Katie looked from Wayne to Steve, "What a wonderful chance for you both."

"Yeah, it'll be great." Steve added, "My life-long dream is not traveling, like Wayne's, but it'll be fun to take that trip."

"Steve is more into sports and studying. He wants to be an engineer."

"I didn't know that," Diana said. "Like your dad, I guess."

Steve nodded. "I've been working in his office this summer. Down there they call me the 'Pick-up Man.'"

"And they aren't referring to girls," Wayne clarified.

"Pick-up man?" Katie asked.

"You know: 'Steve, pick up some coffee', 'Steve, pick up some papers at the printers,' stuff like that."

They talked some more until their pizza arrived and then the boys loaded their plates with three pieces each. They took several bites without saying anything. The girls exchanged grins. Katie leaned across the table toward Diana. "I guess these guys take their food very seriously. I bet there are never leftovers at their house."

"Girls!" Wayne said disgustedly, around a mouthful of crust. "They eat like birds. I could never love a woman who can't down a twelve-ounce steak and a baked potato!"

Diana rolled her eyes. "How boorish!" she quipped.

As the pizza diminished, the talk flourished. It centered on school and sports and the praise band that Wayne played in. He played guitar and led the students in singing during chapel. The spiritual atmosphere was very positive at their school and there was a strong feeling of family among the staff and the student body. Katie was beginning to look forward to being a part of this school. She had always attended Christian schools, but her school in Minnesota had over 900 students. She was warming to the idea of a small high school like this one that had less than 200 kids. Right now, the idea of 'family' felt very good to her. Moving was hard at any time. Moving just before your senior year was terrible. *God, thank you for Diana,* Katie breathed a prayer. *I don't know what I would do without her. Jessica, Lisa and Tami will probably make good friends. And Steve and Wayne...* Katie's stomach did a flip-flop. She looked over at Steve and found his startling blue eyes on her. At her look, he smiled warmly. *And Steve, Lord, will he make a good friend too? A special friend? Is that the reason I had to move here?*

"Earth to Katie," Wayne waved his hand in front of her face. "Are you ready to go?"

Katie shook herself and grinned across the table at Wayne. "You mean you finally finished eating? Aren't you going to order a pizza to go or something? You might need to have a little snack around midnight, don't you think?"

"Girls!" Wayne looked at Steve. "I tell ya, Bro, they always want to organize your life."

"Most guys I know need organizing!" Katie shot back as she swung her legs out from under the table.

Steve raised his hands in surrender. "I'm not even going to go there."

Wayne shook his head and muttered something under his breath as he made his way out.

Diana squeezed Katie's arm. "Score one for you," she whispered with a chuckle.

Out in the parking lot, the boys followed the girls toward Diana's car. Steve reached out and tapping Katie on the shoulder, asked hopefully, "Katie, could I give you a ride home?"

Katie exchanged a look with Diana. Her cousin gave a slight nod. "I'd like that, Steve."

Diana looked at Wayne, "Hey, I'll give you a lift home. You know the saying, 'three's a crowd.'"

Wayne opened the passenger door of Diana's car. "I'd appreciate it, Di, otherwise this brother of mine is going to make me walk home. And it's two miles!"

"That's okay, Wayne," Diana assured him. "We security blankets have to stick together. You know, you're looking a little frayed around the edges. Maybe it's time for Steve to let you go."

Steve and Katie could hear Wayne's howl of laughter as he shut the car door behind him. Diana waved to them and then climbed into the car on her side.

Steve turned to Katie. "What was all that about blankets?"

Katie giggled. "You don't want to know. At least, I'm not going to tell you."

Steve motioned to his Chevy truck, which was parked a little farther down the lot. He had a warm feeling in his heart. *Wayne was right. There is something special about this girl. I wonder if my hair is standing on end?* He chuckled to himself. Noticing Katie giving him a curious look, he smiled at her, dimples appearing on his cheeks. Opening the truck door, he motioned Katie to slide in, and then he walked around to the driver's side.

After he started the truck's engine, he turned to Katie. With his blue eyes sparkling, he said, "I think I agree with Diana."

"About what? Wayne being frayed around the edges?"

Steve grinned. "Well, maybe that too. No," his voice softened, "about what she said last night at the Dairy Shack. About this being the start of something special." Katie blushed as he gazed at her. "Can I see you again sometime?" he asked.

"I think I'd like that," Katie answered. "I think I'd like that a lot."

Chapter 3

A KNIGHT IN SHINING ARMOR

On Tuesday afternoon, the week before school was to start, Katie sat on a folding chair alone in the school guidance counselor's office. While she waited for Mr. Larson to return with a copy of the class schedule they had worked out for her, she glanced around the walls at the posters promoting various Christian colleges, universities and branches of the armed service. Katie shuddered. It was all she could handle right now, to think of which classes to take at a new school this year, without thinking about post-high school. More changes. *I'll have to think about it sooner or later*, she thought. *I wonder what colleges Steve is considering. Now why did I think of him before Diana?* Katie scolded herself and then she realized she had been thinking about Steve often lately. He had asked if he could see her again, but that had been Friday night and she hadn't heard anything from him since then. A sense of panic filled her. *Maybe he thought about it some more and realized he doesn't like me after all.*

The door opened and Mr. Larson entered his office. "All right," he announced with a smile, "I have those copies for you." He handed a small stack of papers to Katie. "I am pleased at how many of your courses transfer into our system. I realize it will be an adjustment here for you, coming from a much larger high school. We just can't offer as many electives as you are used to, but it looks like we've filled your schedule pretty well."

"Thank you, Mr. Larson," Katie said as she gathered her things and stood up. "I appreciate you seeing me today."

"One more thing, Katie. I'd like to encourage you to take part in some extra-curricular activities. I know you said you don't play sports, but it's important that you get involved in something. I recognize the fact that it can be tough to come into a new school your senior year. You might want to think about the drama club or the yearbook staff or, if you like to write, the school newspaper."

"I'll think about it, Mr. Larson. I know you're right. I was on the newspaper staff at my old school. Maybe I could do that again. When are sign-ups for stuff like that?"

"That all takes place the first week of school. Daily announcements are read in your homeroom. Just pay attention to them. By the way, I know your cousins attend school here. Have you had the opportunity to meet any other students yet?"

Katie felt herself blushing. "I've met a few. Some of Diana's friends." *And a certain guy and his brother.*

"Good," Mr. Larson nodded and sat down at his desk. Katie felt that this was her dismissal so she turned to leave. "Thanks again," she called over her shoulder.

"Anytime you need anything, feel free to stop in."

"I will." Katie walked slowly down the school hall, looking around as she went. She peeked into a couple of rooms that had windows in the doors. Computer lab, library, home economics room. As she headed out the front door of the building Katie thought, *I better arrive with Di the first morning. I sure hope we have our first class together.* Worrying about this, she began to dig through the papers Mr. Larson had given her to find her class schedule. Locating it toward the bottom of the stack, she pulled it out. Six other papers came out with it and blew away in the breeze. *Oh bother!* Katie managed to plant her foot down on the nearest one. Bending to retrieve it, she heard a familiar voice.

"These don't belong to you, by any chance, do they?"

She looked up to see Steve holding two sheets of paper while he dashed after a third. "Yes," Katie laughed, chasing after the last two errant papers. Picking them up, she headed over to Steve who had managed to save her school map before it disappeared under a parked green truck.

"I'm really glad I didn't have to crawl under Mr. Larson's truck for these," Steve's blue eyes twinkled as he handed Katie's papers to her. "But for you, I'd do anything."

"A real knight in shining armor." Katie curtsied as she took her papers. "I thank you, Sir." Katie noticed the soccer cleats dangling over Steve's shoulders. He was wearing shorts, shin guards and a t-shirt sporting an athletic logo. "Let me guess," she continued, "soccer practice, right?"

"Yeah, we started yesterday. We practice from three to five. You can hang around and watch if you want to."

Katie peered up at him, questioningly. "People do that?"

Steve shrugged. "Sometimes. Parents. Boy-crazy cheerleaders. Girlfriends. Wayne."

"Wayne watches you practice?"

"Sure, sometimes. He just likes to be around me, I guess. Most people do."

"Oh, you!" Katie playfully swatted his arm.

"Hey, seriously," Steve changed the subject. "I'm glad I ran into you. I had tried to call you before I left home, but your mom said you were out."

Katie's heart skipped a beat. *He had tried to call.*

"I'm really busy this last week of vacation," Steve continued. "I'm working and there's practice every afternoon." He shifted his weight. "But I was wondering, well, Wayne and I were thinking, well, can you hike?"

"Can I hike?" Katie laughed, her green eyes sparkling. "I don't know. What do you have in mind?"

"Well, see, Wayne and I know of this special lake that's great for swimming. It's about an hour's drive from here. It's called Whisper Lake and it has a sandy beach and a few fire pits where we cook supper. There are never very many people there because you have to hike in a mile to get to it. We always go there the last Saturday of vacation for our final summer fling. Do you think you would want to come? You and Diana?"

"Well, I'm sure I can hike a mile, but I'm not sure about doing it with a heavy pack full of food and equipment."

"Aren't you lucky you have your very own knight in shining armor then? Wayne and I have everything we need and we'll carry it in." Steve took a step closer so he was standing directly in front of her.

Other boys began arriving for practice. Car doors were slamming, friends were greeting each other and the coach was pulling a bag of balls from the trunk of his car.

"I have to go. So what do you think? Will you come? And Diana?"

"Yes, for me. I'll check with Di."

"Okay. Good. I'll call you. 'Bye."

Katie watched as Steve jogged toward the soccer field. Another player ran up and slapped him on the back. Katie overheard him tease Steve about his new girl. *Is that what I am? Steve's girl?* Katie smiled and a warm feeling came over her. She wandered a little closer to the field and watched as the guys changed shoes and began to warm up. She had never considered watching a practice. Actually, she had never even seen a soccer game before. Her old school had had a team, but she had never gone to a game. Regretfully she realized she didn't know anything about the rules. *I'll just have to learn. Steve and Wayne can teach me.* With that, Katie turned to leave.

Chapter 4

MILADY

Thursday afternoon found Katie running an errand for her mom. Registration materials for the Christian grammar school her sister would be attending needed to be dropped off before 4:30. Rachel's new school was only a couple of miles beyond Katie's new high school, so although Katie did not know her way around town very well yet, she followed her mother's written directions and managed to find her way to the school and drop off the necessary paperwork in plenty of time.

Now, heading home, Katie hummed along with the radio. She glanced at her new school as she drove past, wondering what it would be like next week when classes started. About a mile down the road, Katie's car started pulling to the right. She turned hard to the left on the steering wheel, but the car kept veering to the right side. Katie's heart began hammering in her throat. Her car had never acted this way before and she wondered if it had a flat tire. She hated mechanical stuff. Katie managed to pull up against the curb and turning off the engine, hopped out to look at her tires. Out of habit, she automatically pushed the lock button on the car door just before slamming it shut. She walked around the car and discovered she did indeed have a flat. Katie desperately looked around, but did not see gas stations or auto shops in the immediate area. Looking back down the road, she remembered passing mostly houses. Deciding to walk ahead to a store to call her dad, Katie reached to open the car door to get her purse. Realizing she had locked herself out, Katie felt like screaming. She could see her keys dangling from the ignition and her purse on the passenger seat in plain sight. The windows were only open a crack. Katie leaned against the side of her car and struggled to remain calm.

She did not know the neighborhood and she had no money in the pocket of her blue shorts for a phone call, even if she could find a phone. Considering her options, she decided to walk the mile or so back to her school. Surely, a secretary or a teacher would be there. If they could not help her, at least they would let her call her dad. Katie looked down at her feet. She was wearing yellow flip-flops. Not the best shoes for walking. Resolutely, Katie began the trek to her school. After about eight blocks, her feet were hurting and her mind had begun to fill with crazy ideas. *What if someone breaks in and steals my purse? The keys! What if someone breaks in, fixes the tire and steals my car?* Katie started to jog. A strap broke on one of her flip-flops causing her to stumble. Catching herself before she fell flat on her face, she yanked both flip-flops off her feet and hurried down the hot sidewalk barefoot. She was sweating and perspiration trickled down the back of her yellow shirt. She glanced at her watch. It was nearly five o'clock. Katie started to worry about no one being at school. *It's still summer vacation. Why would anyone be working this late? Please, Lord, let somebody be there!* Tears began to run down Katie's face and panic rose in her heart.

Finally, she saw the roof of the school gymnasium. Running faster, Katie rushed to the front doors of the school. Locked. She pounded on them. Peering through the window, she realized the halls were dark. Katie turned around and slumped against the door. *Now what?* She began to cry again.

Katie forced herself to calm down and think. Breathe deeply and think. *Wait a minute. Soccer practice.* When she had seen him on Tuesday, Steve had told her that he would have practice every afternoon from three to five this week. She glanced at her watch. It was several minutes after five. *Oh please, God! Let somebody still be here!* Katie ran around the building to the back parking lot, wincing as her bare feet hit the gravel. Only a few vehicles remained in the lot, but thankfully, Steve's red and white Chevy truck was one of them. Katie looked toward the soccer field. There were only three players left on the field. One was in the goalie box, so she assumed it was Steve. One of the other two kicked a ball his way. She watched as Steve dove on it as it headed toward the corner of the net. Katie quickly hobbled the rest of the way across the gravel lot until she reached the grassy field. She looked up again to see that the boys were walking toward their vehicles. She called out, waved and began to jog in their direction.

Noticing her, the boys turned and headed her way. As they neared, Steve recognized her. Quickly, he closed the distance between them. Taking in her tear-streaked face, messy hair and distressed look, he dropped the soccer ball. "Katie! What's happened?" he asked, concern filling his voice.

Katie let her flip-flops fall to the ground and, trying to regain her breath, sobbed out, "My car! The keys! My tire! My purse! Ooh, my feet!"

The two other boys joined Steve. Katie did not know one of them, but recognized the taller sandy-haired one because he had been at the Dairy Shack with Steve and Wayne last week.

Steve put his hands on Katie's arms. "Okay, Katie, relax. I'm here. Slow down and tell us what's happened."

Katie sniffled, took a deep breath and paused a moment to collect her thoughts. She explained the circumstances to the boys, but by the time she got to the part about the school doors being locked and her feet hurting so badly, she began to cry again.

Steve's heart was racing. "John," he said to his friend, "go see if Coach is still in his office. His car is still here, so I would guess he is. Borrow his school keys and bring me a hanger from the Lost and Found. Could you bring Katie a drink of water, too?" As John took off running, Steve turned to the other boy, a younger teammate. "Scott, I know your grandma's waiting for you. You go ahead. John and I will take care of this."

With a last look at Katie, Scott headed over toward his grandmother's brown Impala. Steve took a step closer to Katie. "It's okay," he said soothingly. He did not know quite what to make of all the tears and fuss, but he knew her obvious vulnerability made him feel protective of her.

Katie put a hand over her face as her tears subsided. "I'm so embarrassed. It was all so stupid of me to lose my head like that."

"No, Katie, it wasn't. You're in a strange town, with no money on hand, and not sure where to go," Steve paused, and looked down at her feet and the broken flip-flops laying next to them. "And besides, you had really bad shoes on," he finished in a teasing manner.

Katie lowered her hand, gave Steve a watery smile and sighed. "Once again, you get to be my knight in shining armor."

"I think I'm starting to like this role," Steve responded, now openly grinning at Katie. He looked down at her flip-flops again and raised his eyebrows. "I do have a question for you, though. Why would you wear those things when you're not at the beach?" Steve asked with genuine interest. He really did not understand girls.

"Well, I was just hanging out at home when my mom sent me off in a rush on an errand. I wasn't exactly planning to walk a mile."

John returned with a paper cup filled with water and a wire coat hanger. "Where's your car?" he asked, handing the water to Katie.

She pointed in the general direction as she took a long drink. "A mile or so that way. Thanks for the water, it tastes great."

John nodded a 'you're welcome' and asked, "Do you have a spare in your trunk?"

Katie looked from John to Steve. "I don't know. Would I?"

Steve closed his eyes and tilted his head back. He shook it slowly and grinned. "Come on, John. I'll take Katie with me; you can follow us in your car." Steve bent over and picked up his soccer ball and Katie's flip-flops. They walked to the edge of the grassy field where Steve stopped and turned to her. "Do you want to wear these or go bare foot?"

Katie looked across the parking lot to Steve's truck. It was gravel all the way. While she debated, Steve said, "Never mind. Wait here." He took off jogging toward his truck. He started the engine, drove around the lot and stopped next to where Katie stood. He leaned over and pushed open the passenger door. "Milady?" he invited her into his truck.

When they reached her car, they found everything as she had left it. John worked on getting the driver's door unlocked with the coat hanger, while Steve got tools from his truck and began to take off the flat tire. Katie sat on the sidewalk next to Steve and watched him work.

"Didn't your dad ever teach you how to do this, Katie?" he asked her.

Katie raised her eyebrows. "*My* dad? I'm not sure *he* knows how to do that."

"Every girl should know how to change a tire," Steve stated philosophically.

"That might be true," Katie agreed coyly, "but then we really wouldn't have any need for, say, a knight to come to our rescue."

Steve pulled off the tire and set it down next to the car. He turned and studied Katie. His heart was beating wildly in his throat. She sat there, helpless and so pretty, even with her long, blond hair disheveled and her face still puffy from tears. His mind was muddled and he could not even think of a comeback. "John?" he called, tearing his eyes away from Katie, "you get that door opened yet?"

"Coming!" John was just grabbing the keys from the ignition. He went around the car and opened the trunk. He found the spare tire under an old blanket and carried it around to Steve. "What do you think?"

Steve looked it over as he set it in place. "It'll probably get her home. She lives over by Greenwood."

"Maybe you should follow her," John suggested.

"My thoughts exactly. Thanks a lot, John. I can get it from here."

"Okay," John looked at Katie. "By the way, I'm John. Nice to meet you." He nodded toward Steve. "Guess I'll go now. Take it easy."

"Thank you, John. You guys are so sweet," Katie said gratefully.

John waved away her thanks and headed to his car, leaving Steve to finish tightening the bolts on Katie's wheel.

"Okay," Steve said, standing, and dusting off his hands, "that's it." He picked up the flat tire and tossed it into Katie's trunk. Returning his tools to his truck, he said, "I'm going to follow you home, Katie. I'm not real confident that this tire can make it."

"Please stay for supper," Katie said impulsively. "My mom was making a pan of lasagna when I left and I know she'll want you to stay."

"Okay, that sounds good. Let's stop at my house first so I can shower. You can call your mom from there. I just live a few blocks from here. Let's go in my truck, then swing back around for your car later." Steve reached into Katie's car and grabbed her purse off the seat. He handed both her purse and keys to her as he locked the car doors.

They entered his house through the back door. Steve showed Katie a small half bathroom where she could freshen up a bit before he led her to the kitchen. Mrs. Anderson was standing at the sink, peeling potatoes. Steve introduced her to Katie, briefly explaining about her flat tire and the invitation for supper at Katie's house. He munched on a cookie while Katie phoned home.

"All set?" he asked as Katie hung up the receiver.

"Yes, my mom was getting worried. She was afraid I was lost."

"Where are the boys?" Steve asked his mom. "Katie can hang with them while I shower."

With a smile, his mom indicated the family room, so Steve led Katie down a short hallway. As soon as they left the kitchen, they began to hear boyish laughter. When they entered the room, they saw Wayne laying on his back in the middle of the floor, with two younger boys sitting on him. David, eleven, sat on Wayne's chest, while Adam, the youngest, sat on his feet. The little boys were giggling and Wayne was moaning. Spotting Steve and Katie entering the room, he moaned harder. Winking at Katie, he said, "Ah, an angel of mercy! Hey, Bro," he looked at Steve, "see what happens when you're not here? They're getting so strong I can't fight them off by myself anymore."

Katie giggled at the silliness of that statement. She was sure that Wayne, with his muscular build and broad shoulders, was strong enough to take on both his little brothers, plus one or two of their friends.

Adam laughed harder and tickled Wayne's stocking feet.

"Well, what are we going to do about that?" Steve growled and leaned over Adam's head. He reached out and lightly pinched David in the stomach and then, swiftly, picked Adam up and turned him upside down.

Katie laughed a tension-releasing laugh. "I can help, too, Wayne." She knelt down next to David and began tickling him in the ribs. David, laughing, rolled off his big brother. "Okay, okay, stop!" he spat out between bursts of laughter.

Wayne stood up. "Surrender!" he ordered his brothers.

"Okay, yes!" Adam called, as he hung upside down from Steve's arms.

Steve carefully set his brother down, and Katie stopped tickling David. "Who are you?" David asked her.

"Her name is Katie," Steve announced. To Katie, he said, "This squirt is Adam, that's David."

"Are you Steve's girlfriend?" Adam questioned with curious innocence.

Steve picked Adam up again and swung him over his shoulders. "That, my brother," he scolded, though in a teasing manner, "is a very personal question!"

"Okay, okay, put me down." After Adam was back on his feet, he piped up again. "But what is she doing here?"

"She was over by school. She had a flat tire and I changed it for her. I'm going to shower now and then go to her house for supper. OKAY, Mr. Nosy?" Steve grinned at Adam. "Do you think you guys can entertain her while I'm upstairs without asking any more embarrassing questions?" Steve shot a look at Wayne, with his eyes asking Wayne to watch out for Katie.

"I can," Wayne said, "but maybe these two should go do their homework."

"Wayne," David whined, "school hasn't even started yet!"

"Oh, right," Wayne waved Steve upstairs.

"Do you have any brothers?" David asked Katie.

"I have a sister. I bet she's about your age."

"Yuck." David said. "Come on, Adam, let's go ride bikes until supper."

Wayne and Katie watched the younger boys exit the room. "They are so cute," Katie said.

"You can feel proud. You survived the first Adam/David meeting."

Katie sank down in a brown leather armchair. "That was nothing after the day I've had."

Wayne got them each a cola from the kitchen and they chatted amiably while waiting for Steve. Wayne asked Katie about her family and told her a little of what it was like to live in the Pacific Northwest. They did not get much snow, except in the mountains, but instead had plenty of gray, rainy days in the winter. Wayne's favorite part of the region was the great hiking and biking trails. He sat forward on the couch in his eagerness to share his thoughts with Katie. "I love the outdoors. I jog for exercise, but I really love to hike. On Saturday, when you come along to Whisper Lake, it will just be a short, mile hike. I really like to do longer ones. How about you?"

Katie smiled lightheartedly at him. "I love the wind and puffy white clouds. I love icicles that hang from the eaves like we get in Minnesota, and sunsets and the warmth of the sun." She cocked her head. "You get the picture, right? I love nature, but I don't think I'm what you would call the 'outdoorsy' sort."

"If you hang around with Steve and me long enough, that'll change. I'm glad that Steve plays an outdoor sport. I would hate to think of us spending that many hours each season in a gym."

Steve returned downstairs dressed in clean jeans and a red t-shirt with the phrase 'No Gain; No Pain' written across the front. He and Katie left and, after retrieving her car, he followed her the few miles to the Fremont's home without mishap. Pastor and Mrs. Fremont could not thank Steve enough for helping with Katie's flat tire. Katie's eleven-year-old sister, Rachel, stared at him wide-eyed all during supper. Occasionally, Steve tried to engage Rachel in conversation, but she would only nod or shake her head. When she got up to help her mother clear the table, Steve leaned toward Katie who was sitting beside him and, grinning, whispered in her ear, "Hasn't your sister ever seen a guy before?"

Katie laughed and said quietly behind her hand so her dad would not overhear, "Not one with such blue eyes, I'm thinking. Rachel's at the age where a dashing, older high school boy takes her breath away."

Steve blushed. "Life would probably be easier without younger brothers and sisters embarrassing us, huh?"

"Tit for tat," Katie replied softly, her green eyes sparkling. "I survived meeting your little brothers, now its your turn to deal with Rachel."

After dessert, Steve and Katie played a game of cards with Rachel who continued to eye Steve with open admiration. Rachel's stares made him uncomfortable so he tried not to look her in the eyes too often. Katie smiled good-naturedly, but periodically gave Rachel a poke under the table. She did not want her younger sister scaring Steve away.

Losing the game, Steve looked at Katie. "Do you want to take a walk?"

"That sounds wonderful." Looking at Rachel, she added, "Would you put the game away, please?"

Escaping out the front door, Steve and Katie decided to walk around the block. Siblings aside, Steve knew he enjoyed spending time with Katie. It was going to take more than embarrassing questions and being stared at all night to keep him away. "I'm glad it was me," he spoke up, as they turned onto the sidewalk in front of her house.

"What? The person to lose the game? I thought you let Rachel win on purpose."

"Was it that obvious?"

"Not to her," Katie assured him.

"Good. No, I meant, I'm glad it was me there at school to rescue you today. I think I would feel jealous if some other guy had been the one to change your tire."

"I'm glad it was you, too. Why were you still there, anyway, when most of the other guys were already gone?"

"Oh, John and Scott had this bet going. They wanted to see if I could block ten out of ten shots on goal."

Katie looked up at him with wonder in her face. "Did you?"

Steve shrugged. "Naw, I missed one."

They walked on in silence. Steve felt a desire stirring in him to hold Katie's hand. He had never held a girl's hand before, had never wanted to, but there was something special about Katie. He thought about it some more, and then said, "Do you think it's odd how we keep running into each other? I mean, first at the Dairy Shack last week. It wasn't even a weekend, but we both ended up there. Then, Tuesday, at school when your papers were blowing all over. Then, today."

"I don't believe in coincidences," Katie said, turning to catch Steve's eye. "I honestly believe God has a hand in things like that. I prayed that someone would be at school to help me…He sent you."

"I don't believe in coincidences either." Gaining confidence from Katie's words, he reached over and gently took her hand in his as they continued walking. Her hand felt good in his. It felt small too. Right then, Steve promised himself and God that he would never intentionally hurt this girl.

"Thank you for not sharing all the myriad of details about what happened to me today with our families. I mean, about locking my keys and purse in the car, and the sore feet," Katie said quietly. "And all the crying I did," she added with a small smile as she recalled her earlier unguarded behavior.

Steve squeezed her hand. "They don't need to know all that stuff, Katie. I knew you were embarrassed about it. I wasn't going to make it worse for you."

She smiled at him gratefully. "You really do have this knight thing down pat, Steve Anderson. One would almost think you have done it before."

He looked at her, his blue eyes sparkling. "No, Katie Fremont. You are the only girl I have ever called 'Milady.'" To himself, he added, *You are the first, and I'm hoping you'll be the last.*

Chapter 5

WHISPER LAKE

Late Saturday morning, Wayne pulled his car up next to an old pickup in the dirt parking lot at the trailhead to Whisper Lake. A large branch from a fir tree swept across the roof of the car. "Here we are. Everybody out."

Steve popped opened the trunk and grabbed out a large green backpack. He loosened the top cord and opened the bag.

"Milady," he bowed to Katie. "Please give me your belongings so I may carry them on this mile trek for you."

"Thank you, Kind Sir." Katie handed him a towel, sweatshirt and a new pair of blue flip-flops. "I have the rest of what I need right here." She patted her fanny pack.

Steve looked at the flip-flops in his hand and grinned. Leaning close he whispered, "I'm glad you aren't planning to hike in these things today."

Katie made no reply, but her green eyes glittered and she smiled at him in response to their private joke.

"Hey, Diane," Wayne said. "Where's your stuff? You want me to carry it?"

Diana wadded up her towel, muttering to herself, "Always a buddy, never someone's lady."

"What's that you said?" Wayne asked over his shoulder, hoisting his pack onto his back. "Just stuff your things down in here." He slammed the trunk and pocketed his keys. "You guys all set? The trail head is over here." With that said, he led the way. Steve reached for Katie's hand and gently pulled her after him as he followed Wayne up the trail.

Diana shrugged and fell in line. She tripped over a tree root almost immediately and nearly fell. Katie glanced back. "Are you all right?"

"Fine, fine!" Diana waved. "Don't worry about me." A twinge of bitterness echoed in her voice.

Katie whispered to Steve for him to go on ahead a bit and she waited for her cousin to catch up. At this point the trail through the woods was wide enough for two people so she put her arm around Diana's shoulders and walked next to her.

"Di, is something wrong? Are you okay?"

"Look, Katie, I love you, okay? Steve is a great guy. I told you that from the first and I'm very glad you two are becoming a couple. And Wayne, there," she nodded up ahead. Wayne, his brown hair perpetually a little messy, was whistling as he walked. "He's another great guy. A dream, if you must know, but he doesn't know that I exist. Why am I here? Must I always be a security blanket?"

Katie stopped them in their tracks, turned to look Diana in the eye and put her hands on her shoulders. "Diana, you are my very favorite cousin and my very best friend. Steve likes you and Wayne likes you, too." Katie raised her hand at the look on Diana's face. "Okay, I'll be honest. It doesn't seem like he's falling in love with you, but I know he's falling in 'like' with you. He thinks you're funny. You make him laugh. If Steve and I get serious about each other, can't the four of us be friends together? Wouldn't you like that, really? We could be a group, like the three musketeers, except there would be four of us. We can be there for each other through all the good times and the bad times, too. You know how the Bible says 'a cord of three strands in not easily broken'? Think how strong we could be together with four of us."

"It sounds so nice, Katie," Diana said wistfully.

"Look, none of us know where this relationship is going." Katie glanced up the trail and saw Steve at the bend ahead. He was sitting on a fallen log along the side of the trail, legs spread out in front of him, fiddling mindlessly with a twig. He had his eyes on the girls and when Katie looked his way, he raised his eyebrows and smiled. Katie tightened her hold on Diana's shoulders and looked back into her cousin's dark brown eyes. "I just know I want you to come along with me on this journey I'm starting."

Diana hugged Katie and said softly, "One for all, and all for one."

"Yes!" Katie agreed. "And, please, no more security blanket jokes."

Diana grinned. "Don't take all my fun away, Kate. I can get a lot of miles out of that one yet. Come on," she said, breaking free from Katie's hold. "The guys are waiting, at least your knight is."

Katie fell in step with her cousin as they headed up the trail toward Steve. "Di," she said, "there is one thing I've been wondering. Why does Wayne call you Diane?"

Diana shrugged. "I don't know. It started when we were in middle school. I don't remember the circumstances, but it doesn't bother me. He's the only person that calls me that. In a way, I like it. I guess it makes me feel special." Diana began to hum as they walked, her mood brightening.

Several minutes later, panting, the girls crested the top of the trail just a few feet behind the boys. They watched in amazement as Wayne and Steve dropped their packs to the ground, and then performed some kind of synchronized jig followed by a complicated handshake routine. Diana leaned toward Katie and giggled, "If I hadn't just seen that, I would never believe it!"

Wayne opened his pack and began taking items out and laying them on the ground at his feet. He handed a waterproof bag to Steve, who dropped it a couple of feet out into the lake. Steve then found a rock to weigh it down.

"What...?" Diana exchanged a look with Katie.

"It's our fridge," Wayne explained. "You don't want warm pop and rotten meat, do you? Here," he tossed Diana a tightly folded black plastic ring. "You can blow up the inner-tubes."

Diana moaned and began unfolding hers. "Now I know why they wanted me to come along," she said to Katie. "You'd better watch out, girl, you'll be next."

"Here's another," Wayne threw a blue tube in Katie's direction.

Diana shot her an 'I-told-you-so' look.

"Yep," Wayne stood up and flexed his muscles. "We pack 'em, you fill 'em. Hmm…" he said, stroking his chin, "maybe I should have that printed up on a t-shirt."

Steve looked up from laying out supper supplies, newspaper and fire starter. "Girls, what are you doing?"

"Your pack-it-in partner gave us this job," Diana held her finger over the air hole in the inner tube.

Steve frowned at Wayne. "Wayne," he scolded.

"Oh, all right." Wayne smiled mischievously. He dug deeper into his pack and drew out a small air pump. Shrugging, he said, "I thought it was funny."

"AH!" Diana screeched in disbelief. She jumped to her feet, ran over to Wayne and began to whip him with her partially blown up tube. Wayne laughed, and throwing his hands up in mock defeat, fell good-naturedly to the ground.

Katie chuckled at Wayne's prank and then her expression changed to one of amazement as she took in the assortment of things spread about on the ground next to Wayne. "I just cannot believe all the stuff that came out of that pack." She shook her head in disbelief as she walked over to Wayne's pack and picked up the pump. "Let's get going, cousin, I'm hot and I want to get out on the lake."

The foursome had a great afternoon. They virtually had the lake to themselves. There were only two other men there and they were across the lake fishing from a portable raft. The friends swam, sunbathed, loafed on the inner-tubes, played football keep-away, had camel fights in the water and through it all they laughed often.

As the afternoon wound down, Diana told the others she had had enough of the water. She walked up to shore and found a log not too far from the water's edge. She draped her towel over it, sat down and leaned against it. She watched the other three as they played basketball by trying to toss the football into an inner tube. As far as she could tell, there was a lot of cheating going on, but then the rules were made up and constantly changing. After a while, it became clear that Steve and Katie had teamed up against Wayne. He stuck it out for a while and then gave a high-five to both Steve and Katie. "Good game," he said, "but I've had enough." He grabbed his towel and approached Diana. "Mind if I share your log?"

Diana swept her arm across the open space next to her. "Be my guest."

Wayne opened a side pocket of his pack and fished out two candy bars. He handed one to Diana then settled in next to her. They ate their snack while watching the other two on the lake.

Steve and Katie each climbed onto a tube so they were sitting with their legs and arms dangling over the sides. They linked their feet so as not to float away from each other and talked. They kept their voices low so the two on the beach would not hear. They talked about their families and memories from growing up. They shared dreams and talked at length about Katie's old school and friends. She learned that Steve was a serious and goal-driven young man, but that he was also very tender, sympathetic and a good listener.

Diana and Wayne sat in companionable silence, lost in their own thoughts. The unspoiled surroundings lent an air of quiet and peace that almost lulled them to sleep. Suddenly Wayne's deep voice penetrated Diana's daydreams. "He's falling fast, and he's falling hard."

Diana looked over at Wayne and followed his gaze to the water, where Steve and Katie still floated. They had drifted out a little farther but she could still hear Katie's soft laughter. "Katie's never been in love before," Diana shared confidentially. "She's dated a little bit, but it was never anything serious. Never anything meaningful."

"Same with Steve. He never wanted a girl in his life. Always said it would complicate things. I hope this works out for them. They make a good couple."

"You don't think there's going to be any pain, do you?"

Wayne looked at Diana. "What do you mean?"

Diana continued to watch the pair on the lake. "Something Katie said to me earlier. She said she wanted us four to be a group. To be there for each other through the good times and the bad times."

"That's just talk," Wayne said in a reassuring manner. "But I do like the sentiment of sticking together."

Diana, eyes focused on her cousin and Wayne's brother, whispered, "One for all, all for one."

"Let's make it a pact." Wayne held out his hand and shook Diana's hand. His voice dropped. "And if there is any pain, you do realize, it will be you and me left to pick up the pieces."

Diana's voice was faint. "Let's pray there isn't." She shivered. "I'm getting cold. Do you know what happened to my sweatshirt?"

"It's over there," Wayne pointed and stood up. "I'll start the fire. My stomach tells me it must be close to suppertime. You want to haul that bag up here from the water?"

Diana and Wayne busied themselves with building a fire and laying out supper supplies. Diana set out hot dogs, buns, pork and beans, chips and apples. "I'm glad to see some fruit here," she teased.

Wayne grunted. "Yeah, Steve insisted. It's a variation on our usual menu."

Diana laughed. "I'll thank him."

Wayne called the other two up from the lake. They came hand in hand from the water's edge. Steve handed Katie her towel and she wrapped her long hair in it. Steve quickly dried off, then handed his towel to Katie, too. They quickly pulled jeans and sweatshirts on over their swimsuits and approached the fire to warm their hands and feet.

"Fabulous fire, Wayne," Katie complimented.

"Yeah, thanks, Bro," Steve agreed.

Wayne tossed Steve the package of meat. "You want to cook?"

After their stomachs were full and the garbage disposed of, Steve stuck a couple more pieces of wood on the fire. He sat down near it and motioned Katie to sit next to him. She took a comb from her fanny pack and began detangling her long hair while she sat. Wayne lifted up his pack and dug into it.

"What more could be in there?" Katie asked Steve.

"Music, my dear," Wayne answered her as he waved his recorder in the air. "I couldn't very well pack my guitar up here, but we can make do with this. Most people only think of recorders as something fourth graders learn to play, but if you know how, you can get some sweet music out of one of these."

He sat down in between the girls and began to play a praise song. When he moved into the second song, Wayne closed his eyes and leaned forward with emotion. Katie could tell from watching and listening to him, that Wayne was passionate, not only about his music, but about his God, too. She heard Steve's tenor voice at her side as he began to sing while his brother played. *"There is a Redeemer…"* Katie had known very few guys at her old school that were so open about their faith. She admired this about these Anderson brothers. She admired that and a whole lot more. They were fun and sweet. Genuine seemed a good descriptive word for both of them.

Diana caught her eye and, with her look, asked Katie to join her in singing along with Steve. The girls raised their voices with his and filled their little area of the beach. Steve reached for her hand and Katie felt that she and Steve were truly one in spirit as they sang. Katie was not sure how long they sat there worshiping God through song, but she was certain it must have been close to an hour before Wayne laid his instrument aside. It was nearing dusk, the shadows of the trees lengthening across the lake.

"As much as I hate to break this mood," Steve announced. "We'd better pack up. We still need some daylight to get down the trail and back to the car."

Katie slowly stood up. "This has been a perfect day. I hate to have it end. You know, I was mad at God when my dad first told me we were moving here, and now…" she wiped a tear from her eye, "now…"

Steve placed an arm around her shoulders. "We understand," he said. "And I'm so glad you're here." Katie laid her head on his shoulder and he put his mouth near her ear. "You are the best thing that ever happened to me," he whispered.

Diana stood up and brushed the grass and dirt from her pants. She tilted her head toward Wayne and said confidentially, "I don't think they need their security blankets anymore. They have each other now."

Wayne shouldered his pack. "Yeah," he agreed, "but you and I are going along for the ride. Remember, one for all…"

"…And all for one," Diana finished.

Chapter 6

MY HEART BELONGS TO YOU

Katie stood in front of the full-length mirror that was attached to her closet door and surveyed herself with a critical eye. She was dressed in a jean skirt, a red and white striped shirt and sandals. Her long blond hair was pulled back in a French braid. First day of school butterflies flittered through her stomach. Hearing the honk of Diana's car horn she grabbed her backpack and scrambled down the stairs.

"'Bye, Mom," she called. She nearly ran into her younger sister at the bottom of the stairs. Rachel's eyes were the same green as Katie's, but her hair, which was shorter and curled around her shoulders, carried a hint of red in its blond locks. "You look cute," Katie complimented. "I know you're worried, but the kids will like you, Rachel. Just be yourself. Sixth grade can be a lot of fun."

"Okay," Rachel said. "You, too. At least you have Diana and Nikki at your school."

"I know." Katie hugged her sister, then poked her head around the corner of the kitchen and exchanged goodbyes with her mother, before she hurried out to Diana's car. She climbed into the front seat and turned to greet her cousins. Nikki sat in the back, chattering excitedly.

"It'll be so fun this year, being a sophomore," she was saying. "Last year I was so scared the first day. Are you scared, Katie?"

"Well, not exactly scared," Katie answered. "Anxious, I guess." Actually, she was not jittery about how this first day of her senior year would go as much as she was wondering what it would be like to see Steve again. She had not seen or talked to him for a few days, not since the day of the hike to the lake. She wondered if he would pay special attention to her in front of their classmates. *Will he walk me to class? Will he sit by me at lunch?* Daydreams of Steve had begun to fill many of Katie's thoughts. She wondered if he really liked her as much as she felt that she liked him. It seemed that way, but then, boys could be so vague sometimes. She pictured his face in her mind, with the dimples that came out when he smiled and his eyes that gorgeous cornflower blue. He was definitely the cutest boy she had ever known.

"Here we are," Diana announced as she pulled into the student section of the school's parking lot. Katie realized she had been daydreaming the entire ride to school and had not heard a word of what her cousins had been saying. "I thought it might be kind of nice to get here a little bit early," Diana continued. "That way you can meet a few kids before we go to the opening assembly in the auditorium."

"You're sweet, Di," Katie said as she opened her car door. A casual glance around the parking lot did not reveal either Wayne's black car or Steve's red and white truck. She smoothed her skirt and took a deep breath. "Here we go."

Katie sat at a desk behind Diana in senior homeroom. Other students were sitting at desks or milling around catching up with friends after the summer vacation. A few kids had come up to meet Katie. Jessica, Lisa and Tami had seemed genuinely glad to see her again. Katie noticed one boy perched on the top of a desk in the back corner of the room. He kept eyeing her and when she looked his way, he saluted her. She smiled at him and exchanged pleasantries with a few kids, but all the while, she kept glancing toward the door, watching for Steve's arrival. She had just met a petite, dark-haired girl name Patti when Wayne appeared in the doorway. He took one step into the room and called out loudly, "Hey, everybody! Did y'all meet Katie?"

Katie blushed and momentarily covered her face with her hands. She looked up in time to see Steve enter the room. Like Wayne, he wore jeans and a t-shirt. He stopped in the doorway and scanned the sea of faces before him. When his eyes met Katie's, he winked.

Katie felt a warmth spread through her body and she smiled back. Steve turned away and strode over to the front corner where some of his friends had congregated. Katie recognized John and one other boy from that night two weeks ago at the Dairy Shack when they had been playing pool with Steve and Wayne.

Mr. Jennings, their math teacher and senior homeroom advisor, entered the classroom. He had to skirt around a few students who had gathered near the chalkboard. Laying his brief case on his desk, he raised his voice above the chatter of students.

"Seats, please," he requested. "I have just a few minutes before the assembly to take roll and make some announcements, but before we open the day with prayer, I want to welcome you back. I understand we have a new student with us." Black reading glasses riding low on his nose, his eyes combed the room until he found Katie. "Katie Fremont, Diana's cousin, I believe. Please make her feel welcome."

The boy from the back corner whistled, causing Katie to blush again. "That will do, Ryan." Mr. Jennings opened his Bible and the class settled down. "Let's spend a few moments in His presence before we take care of business."

"I can't believe it's Friday already," Diana said as she pulled a history book from her locker. "Did you decide what to do for the media project?"

Katie opened her own locker as she answered, "I chose the poetry one. I'm thinking about using Christina Rossetti. What about you?"

"Definitely not poetry. I have a hard time understanding that stuff. I'm leaning heavily toward the television option. I could do a comparison of TV sit-coms. Imagine how fun it would be to watch television for a homework assignment." Diana put the last of what she needed into her backpack. "We should have made plans for tonight. Too bad I have to baby-sit for a neighbor." She leaned closer to Katie so the few surrounding students would not overhear the rest of their conversation. "Has Steve called you yet?"

Katie shook her head and continued to sort through what books she needed at home over the weekend.

"I wonder what his problem is. You haven't said too much about it, but I've noticed that he hasn't paid much attention to you this week. Not like Ryan, who tries to sit by you at every opportunity."

"I know," Katie's words came out softly. "I've tried not to encourage Ryan. I don't know what's going on with Steve, but if there's any hope of a future with him, I don't want to blow it."

Diana slammed her locker shut. "You need to have a talk with him, Katie."

"No, I couldn't. He never actually made any commitment to me."

Diana paused for a moment, thinking. "Maybe so. Okay, I'll talk to Wayne then. He'll know where Steve's head is—or should I say his heart?"

Katie gave Diana a stricken look. "Don't, Di, please. Just let it rest for now."

"Okay, but listen, Katie. I will give him one week. If he hasn't talked to you or made some kind of move by then, I am going to seriously consider talking to Wayne. This isn't fair to you." Diana turned away from the lockers. "If you're ready, let's go."

"No, I can't. You go ahead. I have that interview for the paper."

"What interview is that?"

"Didn't I tell you? My first assignment is to interview the new Spanish teacher. Carrie really wanted to do it, but Mrs. Woods gave the assignment to me."

"Carrie probably wanted to do it because Mr. Karsten is such a dream. I heard that he's fresh out of college. Most likely Carrie wants an excuse to flirt with him. I'll see you later."

Katie pulled a notebook from her locker to use for her interview. She pondered the thought of Mr. Karsten being cute. *Funny, I didn't notice that before,* Katie thought, but she knew why. Sighing, she leaned into her locker and let tears gather in her eyes. The reason stood about five foot eleven with short blond hair and eyes so blue a girl could drown in them. *Why has he been ignoring me all week? Have I lost him before I ever really had him?*

"Katie?" Startled at the sound of Steve's voice behind her, Katie jerked her head back so far she banged it on the open locker door.

"Ouch!" She dropped her books and put her hands on her head. *At least he'll think I'm crying because my head hurts – he doesn't have to know it's my heart that's aching.*

"I'm sorry, Katie." Steve put a hand on top of Katie's head, covering her hands with his larger one. "Are you okay? I didn't mean to scare you."

"It's okay." Katie put her hands down and gave him a watery smile. "Well, it will be okay."

Steve bent down to retrieve her books. "Seems as if we've done something like this before, Milady. Here." He stood, and then handed the pile to Katie. "I need to talk to you, Katie. I have a short practice tonight and I thought maybe you could wait, and then," Steve paused, shifted his weight and then went on, "well, no, I guess you wouldn't want to wait. It's still an hour practice, but I could come by your house after –."

Katie held a hand up, "It's okay. I'll wait. I have an assignment for the school newspaper to work on. I'll be here after practice, waiting for you." She looked into Steve's eyes and felt as if he was trying to memorize every detail of her face. "You better go," her voice caught in her throat, "or you'll be late."

"Yeah," Steve reached out and tentatively touched her cheek. "Sorry about your head. I'll see you later." He turned then and jogged down the hall.

Katie watched until he was out of sight. *Well, Di, I guess we're going to talk.* She straightened her pile of books and squared her shoulders, her heart hammering. She would not allow herself to think about it until after her interview. She needed to focus on that now.

Her interview with Mr. Karsten completed, Katie knew the boys still had a half hour of practice left so she went outside to a picnic table and began to compose an article from her notes. She wanted her first assignment to be perfect. After working diligently for a time, Katie felt she had a good rough draft down on paper. She glanced over toward the soccer field and realized that practice must have ended because some of the boys were heading to their cars. She caught sight of Steve tossing his cleats and other gear into his truck. He shut the door and slowly jogged over to join her. Katie closed her notebook and tucked it and her pen into her daypack.

Steve reached the table and sat down across from her. Opening the conversation, he said, "Thanks for waiting."

"No problem," Katie felt like she was laying her heart on the table for Steve to dissect.

"I know I need to talk to you," Steve confided, "but I don't know how to start."

Katie clasped her hands together to keep them from trembling. "Just say what's on your mind, Steve," she encouraged.

"What's on my mind?" Steve ran a hand through his short hair. "It's you, Katie. You're on my mind. On my mind and in my heart and under my skin. I've never felt this way about any girl before." Steve paused and searched her eyes. "But I don't deserve you. You deserve much better than me."

Katie felt her heart drop to her feet. "No, Steve, I…" She reached out and enfolded one of his hands in her clasp. "Why do you say that?"

Steve looked down at their hands. "It's true. I'm too busy for you and that's not fair to you. I know that girls need to spend a lot of time with their boyfriends. They want to talk on the phone every night and go out places and be together. But, Katie," he looked up, pleading with his eyes for her understanding, "I can't do all that. I have schoolwork and I need to keep my grades up. There's soccer and youth group and Wednesday night Bible study. On Tuesday, I'm going to start tutoring a seventh grade boy from my church. His mom hired me to come twice a week to help him with math. And then there's time with Wayne." Steve drew in a deep breath. Katie started to say something but Steve gently laid the fingers of his free hand over her mouth. "Please let me finish, okay? Katie, I'd have to squeeze you into such little chunks of time and you should have a guy who can be with you all the time and treat you like a queen."

"Steve, you do treat me like a queen," Katie's eyes glistened with unshed tears. "I'm your 'lady', remember? Please don't be saying goodbye."

Steve went on, seeming to ignore her statement. "At the beginning of this week I was really excited to see you, but then I couldn't help noticing how Ryan and Greg and some of the other guys were eyeing you and talking to you, and stuff. At first, I was mad, or maybe jealous, and I wanted to tell them to lay off, that you were *my* girl. Then I realized that you've just moved here and don't know many people. You should have a choice of what guy you spend your time with, not just end up with the first one you met. Some of those clowns could probably treat you a lot better than I can. That's why I backed way off. I'm willing to walk out of your life right now and leave you free if you need a guy who can pay you more attention than I can. I want you to feel free to – to – aw, Katie!" Steve rubbed his temples. "I've made such a mess of things this week."

A tear trickled down Katie's cheek. "Can I talk now?"

When Steve nodded, she came around the side of the table and sat on the bench next to him. The late afternoon sun had sunk behind a line of trees and the table was now wrapped in light shadows. Dressed in lightweight khaki pants and a short-sleeved blue blouse, Katie shivered in the cooler air, but inside her blood ran hot. "Listen to me, please? I'm not like you think. I don't need to talk on the phone every single night or be with you every minute of every day. As long as I know that we're a 'together' thing, it'll be okay. Steve, I'm not the least bit interested in those other guys. I want you. I will take whatever you have to give me, but please don't ignore me at school anymore. Don't let those other guys think that I'm fair game, because my heart already belongs to you."

Steve wrapped an arm around Katie's shoulders. "Katie, I told you last week that you were the best thing that ever happened to me. If you really want me and can take me as I am, then I am yours, Katie Fremont. And I'll let Ryan and those other guys know it, too. I'll shout it from the gym roof, if you want me to."

Katie smiled and wiped her eyes. "I don't think that will be necessary, but maybe you could sit with me at lunch on Monday."

Steve pulled back from the embrace. With a finger, he tilted Katie's face up toward his. "You are wonderful. I promise I'll try not to hurt you again. Come on, it's getting cold out here. Let's go. Maybe you could come over after supper. We could watch a video or something."

"Okay," she replied, "that sounds terrific." Katie's heart soared and her face reflected her happiness. Everything felt right. She grabbed her bag with one hand, and Steve took hold of the other as they walked toward the parking lot.

"It can't be a late night, though," he said. "We have our first soccer game tomorrow. Can you come? Would you want to? It's an away game, but Wayne will be driving his car. You could ride with him."

"I wouldn't miss it," Katie said, squeezing his hand.

Chapter 7

DREAMS

After the first week of school and their talk at the picnic table, Steve and Katie became more secure in their relationship. They did not have a lot of time or opportunity to be together, but they made the most of what they did have. The more they talked, the better they got to know each other which helped deepen their feelings for one another.

The other forty kids in the senior class began to see and accept them as a couple. The boys who had shown an interest in Katie that first week of school gave up the pursuit. All, that is, except for Ryan. He shadowed Katie and grabbed open seats next to her whenever possible.

During lunch hour on a Thursday afternoon in early October, Wayne finally convinced Ryan that what Steve and Katie shared was special. Because the day was warm and sunny, as days tend to be in Western Washington in the early fall, most of the upperclassmen were sprawled on the lawn or eating at picnic tables. Steve and Katie were sitting cross-legged on the edge of the lawn. Steve wore shorts, a Hawaiian t-shirt and tennis shoes. Katie had on jeans, a short-sleeved rugby-style shirt and her sandals. Her blond hair was in a long ponytail that fell halfway down her back. Steve was fishing in his sack lunch, hoping to find more to eat. Katie handed him a baggie of gingersnaps left from her own lunch.

Ryan stood several feet away, leaning against the side of the building. While eating an apple, he intently watched the carefree couple lounging on the grass. Wayne finished his lunch and crumpled up his garbage. Needing to talk to the band instructor, he headed across the lawn toward the trashcan. Noticing Ryan, Wayne followed his gaze and shook his head. He knew Ryan had been bothering Katie and he knew, too, that it made Katie uncomfortable. He approached Ryan and as he tossed his garbage into the can, said, "They only have eyes for each other, you know. It's been that way from the first time they saw each other."

Ryan threw his apple core into the garbage can with more force than was necessary. "You can't blame a guy for trying. There's always hope."

"Not this time. You'd better just accept it. It'll make your life a lot easier."

Ryan looked sharply at Wayne. "Oh, man," he said sympathetically. "You speaking from experience here?"

Wayne looked back over toward Steve and Katie and shrugged. "Whatever. I'm just telling you, you're wasting your time." That said, Wayne strode off in the direction of the music room.

Ryan watched him until he entered the building. "That's a tight spot," he muttered. Briefly mulling over Wayne's advice, he decided to ease up on Katie, but to furtively watch for any future opportunities in case Mr. Straight-A-Soccer-Star could not keep Katie happy. Turning his back on Steve and Katie, he sauntered over to a group of sophomore girls and broke into their conversation.

Steve finished the last of Katie's cookies. "Are you coming to my game today?"

"Of course. You know I only missed that one game when I had that bad cold. Wayne's been great about letting me ride along with him."

Steve stuffed his crumpled wax paper into his brown lunch sack. "Well, he's going to the game anyway, you might as well ride along with him. Mom and Dad make it to most of my games, but in three years, I don't think Wayne has ever missed. You know who else will be there?"

"Tell me."

"Coach said a college coach is gonna show up. He said there was one at Monday's game, too." Steve's blue eyes shown with excitement.

"A coach!" Katie sounded surprised. "College coaches are coming to watch you? Steve, do you want to play soccer in college?"

Steve stretched his legs out in front of him. "Yes, I do. I've been dreaming about that for a couple of years. I didn't say anything to you before, because, well," Steve ran a hand through his short hair, "in case no school wants me, you know."

"You're kidding, right? Of course they'll want you. I admit I don't know much about soccer, but I know you're very good."

Steve grinned at her, his dimples showing. "Well, you might be just a tad biased."

"All right, maybe I am, but I read the newspaper and I hear people talk."

"Oh yeah?" Steve leaned back on his elbows, enjoying the attention. "And what do you hear?"

"Mr. Larson said you're the best goalie this school has ever had. Wayne says you're smart and you're quick."

"Yeah, well," Steve's blue eyes twinkled. "Wayne's biased too."

Katie persisted. "Look at all those shots you blocked Monday. Six!"

Steve nodded. "But I let that one get past me."

Katie poked him with her foot. "I said you were good, not perfect."

Steve chuckled. "A guy's just gotta love ya, Katie," he said lightheartedly, basking a bit in her open admiration.

Katie froze. *A guy's just gotta love ya.* Steve's words echoed in her mind. That was the first time the word love had come up between them. Steve had not even kissed her yet. *Calm down, Katie,* she chided herself, *he's just teasing you.* A quietness settled over the couple. Steve laid all the way back on the grass and closed his eyes. Katie pondered what Steve had shared with her about the special visitor to today's game. After a few minutes, she nudged Steve with her foot to get his attention.

"Yeah? I'm awake."

"Steve," Katie said tentatively, "About this college business; we're going to have to discuss it sometime. Where you're going, where I'm going. What we're going to do."

Steve sat up, his carefree mood gone. He felt like a rock was sitting in his stomach. "I know, I know. We'll figure it out, but there isn't time now." As if on cue, the bell rang. He stood and reached out a hand to help Katie up. "To be honest, at this point, I wouldn't know what to say. I don't know where I'm going next year. I just know that I am going and that I want to play soccer wherever I go."

After a thirty-minute drive to the opponent's school for the afternoon's soccer match, Katie followed Wayne up the bleachers. She settled in next to him and they watched the players finish their warm-ups. The lunchtime conversation with Steve was still on Katie's mind.

"Wayne," she said, "What are you going to do next year? After graduation? Are you going to college? What do you want to do?"

"That's easy, Katie. Travel." Wayne looked off into the distance. "I want to travel around the world. I want to bring my guitar and write songs and share music with the people I meet. I'm not much interested in the tourist traps. I'd like to go off the beaten paths, to the remote areas. I've been thinking that I could share the gospel through my music."

"Like a missionary?"

"Not officially. The problem is, a dream like that takes money. I don't have that part figured out yet." Wayne's eyes traveled the field until they rested on Steve. He watched his brother, his best friend, go through a stretching routine. "Thing is, I had always pictured Steve going with me. From the time we were in fifth grade and started studying world geography, Steve and I have dreamed and talked about seeing the world. Russia, Australia, South Africa, places like that." Wayne paused and seemed so lost in thought that Katie was not sure if he was talking to her anymore or to himself. Then he continued, "But now, Steve's life is going in a different direction. About a year ago, I realized it was all only talk on Steve's part. For me, it's always been real."

"It is a wonderful dream, Wayne," Katie acknowledged. "But

you're right. It's not Steve's dream. It's just yours."

"The real problem for me is that I can't really picture myself going without him. We've always been together. I'm caught in the middle here. I can't see him coming with me, and I can't picture myself going alone..." Wayne sighed. "I guess I haven't given up hope completely yet. Maybe I can still get him to go somewhere with me."

"There's that trip with your uncle."

"Yeah...well, we'll see."

On the field, the players had lined up to start the game. Steve was in the goalie box. "Come on, Bro!" Wayne yelled through cupped hands. "Let's do it again!"

Katie was amazed at how quickly Wayne shifted gears. "I want to thank you again for carting me along to all these away games. I'll have to fill your car up with gas. I can't help but wonder, though, if I'm getting in your way. You know, you might want to take your own girlfriend along."

"No such thing, Katie dear. I don't have a girlfriend and I don't particularly want one. Anyway, you're good company." Wayne took his eyes off the field and studied Katie's profile as she watched the opening moves of the game. "I've enjoyed spending time with you, getting to know my brother's girl." A funny feeling twisted in Wayne's stomach. Pulling his eyes from her, he looked toward Steve, who stood alert, ready for action. "It's the least I can do for Steve. He likes you, Katie, so be good to him."

"I will," Katie promised, her eyes on Steve, even though the play was on the other end of the field.

"Besides, it's been fun watching the game through fresh eyes," Wayne said, his brown eyes glittering. "And if I can get you to understand the off-sides rule by the end of the season, I'll die a happy man."

Chapter 8

FRED & ETHYL

It was a chilly Monday evening in late October. Katie lay on her bed reading a story in her literature book. She was interrupted by her dad's voice calling up the stairs saying that Steve was at the door. She bounced down the steps to find that her dad and Steve had stepped into the living room.

"Steve!" Katie greeted, "What are you doing here?"

"Well," Steve pocketed his truck keys, "I figured out that if I took a round about route to Mark's house for tutoring, then I'd drive right past your house. I got to thinking about that great apple pie your mom had yesterday and I was hoping there might be a piece leftover." Steve's blue eyes were sparkling. "Your dad, here, said he ate the last piece for dessert tonight." Steve shrugged his shoulders. "As long as I'm here and I don't have to be at Mark's until seven-thirty, I might as well stay for a while."

Katie giggled. Her dad motioned to the couch. "Sit here, Son. Katie, I'll be in my study."

Steve took a seat and watched Pastor Fremont until the study door closed behind him. "Where's your mom and sister?" he asked Katie.

"At the mall. Rachel needs a new jacket."

Steve patted the cushion beside him. "Come here," he invited.

"I'm so glad you're here," Katie said, sitting down close by him. "I want to ask you something. Actually, Diana and I want to ask both you and Wayne something."

Steve moaned. "Why do I get the feeling this is not a good thing?

I've noticed that when Diana is involved things can get a little crazy." He was remembering the weekend before when Diana had insisted on doing her home economics assignment with Katie, Wayne and himself as her guinea pigs. Diana's homework was to plan, shop for and prepare a complete three course meal, and keep to a budget. The chili had turned out so spicy that Steve had downed nearly a quart of water with it, then, the blueberry pie was too sour so he'd kept scooping ice-cream onto his plate until he must have eaten a quart of that as well.

"I promise it doesn't involve cooking!"

"That's a relief. Okay, what do you want?"

"Saturday night our youth group is having a costume/bowling party. We're all supposed to dress up like famous couples. There's going to be prizes and everything. Diana and I have come up with the best idea!"

"I can hardly wait to hear this," Steve said dryly.

"How does this sound?" Katie paused for dramatic effect. "Fred and Ethyl and Ricky and Lucy from the 'I Love Lucy' show!" Katie rushed on before Steve could respond, "You know, those four were such good friends—like we are. We can shop at thrift stores for costumes. Diana and I can wear old looking housedresses. Diana's neighbor even has a red wig we can borrow." Katie paused, but Steve didn't say anything. "Well, what do you think?"

"I have one question," Steve drawled. "Who am I? Fred or Ricky?"

"Well, Diana really should be Lucy. She's taller than me and she's funny like Lucy. She fits the part much better than I do, don't you agree?"

"Yep, and next thing you'll tell me is that since Wayne is tall and dark, he fits the Ricky role better."

"Y-e-s. He even plays in a band like Ricky."

"Now that's an important consideration." Steve tried to keep a straight face so Katie would not know he was enjoying himself. "In other words, I look like Fred Mertz."

Katie laughed. "I did not say that! You're not bald at all," she patted his stomach, "or paunchy either."

"So, what do I have to wear?"

"You know, grandpa clothes. And a pillow."

"A pillow?"

"Yes, Steve, to make you look fat. I'll have to wear one too."

"And we have to go out in public like this?"

"Just to the bowling alley and then to the church for pizza afterwards."

"I think I'd rather have another bowl of Diana's chili."

"Oh, come on, Steve, please," Katie pleaded. "Will you do it? Do you think Wayne will?"

"I'm sure Wayne won't take any convincing. I mean, it's no big deal for him, right? He can basically come as his tall, dark, handsome self."

"I know that Fred and Ethyl don't have the same flair as Ricky and Lucy, but it'll be fun, Steve."

"Oh, Katie," Steve put his arm around Katie's shoulders. "Don't you know that I'd do almost anything for you? Yes, I'll be your Fred and you can be my Ethyl."

With that settled, Katie relaxed. "Thank you," she whispered, melting under Steve's intense gaze.

"If we're Fred and Ethyl, then we're married," Steve's voice had turned husky. Gently, he pulled Katie's head closer to his. "And we've been married for a long, long time."

"And we're growing old together," Katie added in a whisper.

"I think I'd like to kiss my wife." Steve's lips tenderly met Katie's. It was a brief first kiss. A moment when time stood still. Steve pulled just far enough away to speak softly. "On Saturday night, you might look like Ethyl Mertz to everyone else, but to me you'll always be Milady." He leaned in and gave Katie one more soft kiss on the lips before pulling back and taking his arm out from around her. He patted her knee and said a little regretfully, "I've got to get to Mark's."

Katie's head was in the clouds and her heart was beating wildly. She had dreamed of this moment for most of her teenage years. She had often tried to picture what it would be like when she received her first kiss. If this first kiss was any indication of what a relationship with Steve was going to be like, she knew it would surpass all of her girlhood dreams. Because of Steve's kiss, she could hardly think straight, but he appeared calm so she wanted to also. Reining in her emotions, she focused on the topic they had been discussing before that unexpected, but long anticipated kiss. "Can you go costume shopping with us this week?"

"No can do," he said, getting up. "We have extra-long practices this week to get ready for our tournament game Friday night. It's going to be so neat, Katie. It'll be down at William's Field under the lights and everything."

Katie loved the way Steve became animated when he talked about soccer, and she loved the way he was tender with her. "And if you win on Friday?"

"Then it's on to the state tournament."

"And if you lose?" Katie almost hated to ask. "Will you be all right?"

"I'll be okay." Steve gently pinched her cheek. "I've got my Ethyl to keep me going." He opened the front door and looked back at Katie. "Just don't buy too big of a pillow for my stomach, okay?"

Katie laughed as she shut the door behind him. She leaned against it and closed her eyes. Her knight in shining armor had given her her first kiss. It was the sweetest moment in her life. One she knew she would remember forever.

Saturday night the costume/bowling part was a success. Steve, Katie, Wayne and Diana arrived at the bowling alley not only in costume, but in character as well. Katie had a scarf tied over her hair and Steve was wearing an old angler's hat. Diana kept them laughing all night as she tried to act like Lucy. She dropped her bowling ball and one time sent it rolling so crazily down the alley that it bounced over the gutter and landed in the next lane. The group broke down in laughter, but Wayne said in an aside to Steve, "I'm not really sure that was part of her act. Diane's a bit crazy herself."

At the end of the evening, when the winners for the best famous couple were announced, Wayne and Diana took first place. They went up to the front of the room to receive their prizes, coupons to the Dairy Shack. Katie watched, standing next to Steve, his arm around her shoulder. She was so happy for the positive attention Diana was receiving. For herself, she had all she needed with her knight in shining armor.

Steve leaned his head toward Katie. "Lucy may be taking first place with the judges, but Ethyl will always be first place with me." He brushed her cheek with a quick kiss.

"Why, Mr. Mertz," Katie said, as her breath caught in her throat, "you could turn a girl's head with such sweet talk."

"That's nothing," he responded, "you, Milady, have turned my whole world upside-down."

Chapter 9

CHRISTMAS LOCKET

October turned to November, November to December. Katie found herself in the little side room off the school art room collating copies of the latest edition of the school newspaper. Two fellow staff members, Brian and Amy, would be joining her soon. Katie had a study hall, so she had decided to get an early start. After collating, they would need to fold the papers and count them out for homeroom delivery the next morning.

Katie paused in her sorting, to view again the article Brian had written about the success of the soccer team. They had taken second place at the state tournament. It was a first in the history of the school to even make it to the state competition. Everyone agreed that the whole team had played well, but that Steve had played the best game of his high school years. Along with the article, Brian had included a photo of the team and one of Steve wearing his orange goalie shirt. The caption under the picture of Steve read "Goalie; Captain; Champ." Katie knew that she would cut out that photo and article and place them in her scrapbook, or she could even buy a frame and have it matted for her bedroom wall. Maybe she would do one for Steve, too, and give it to him for Christmas. That would solve her dilemma of what gift to buy for him.

Mulling over the possibilities of Christmas and vacation from school, Katie began to wonder if finally during this upcoming school break she and Steve could actually find a large chunk of time to spend together. She knew all about the debate of quality vs. quantity where spending time with loved ones was concerned. She could not really find fault with the quality of time spent with Steve, because he always managed to make her feel special, even in the midst of a crowd. Katie had to admit, however, that most of their dates involved other people; usually Wayne, frequently Diana; more often than not, some of the guys from the soccer team, especially John. Even so, Steve had a way of catching her eye across a crowded table at the Pizza Ranch or across a room at school and saying with his look how much he cared for her. *If only it could happen more often. If only we did not have to squeeze our times together into little portions, working around Steve's crazy schedule.*

As Katie's thoughts wandered, and her hands kept busy with the sorting, she heard voices in the art room as some students wandered in. She could tell that they went directly over to the cupboards and were getting down jars of poster paint.

"What do these posters need to say?" Katie noted that it was Jessica speaking.

"Just a reminder about ticket sales for the Christmas banquet. They need to have a final count by the end of school on Wednesday, and Mike says there aren't very many sold yet."

Katie clearly recognized Tracy's voice despite the wall between them. Her hands stilled as she cocked her head. She had left the door to the little side room open and she could easily overhear the conversation coming from the art room. *Christmas banquet! That's right. I need a ticket. Won't Steve buy me one?* It was Monday afternoon. Tickets had been on sale for nearly a week already. Tracy had just said there were only two days left in which to buy them. *Why hasn't Steve talked to me about this? Isn't he planning to take me?* Confused thoughts swirled through Katie's mind, as the dialogue in the next room continued.

"Tracy, you are so lucky that Mike asked you. So many of the guys go stag."

"Or else they wait until almost the last minute," Lisa piped up. "I don't understand. Are they afraid of us, or what? Now is the time it would be nice to have a steady boyfriend, like Katie. You wouldn't have to wait and wonder for a whole week if some guy is going to ask you and then end up buying your own ticket at the last minute."

Katie could almost smile, if it were not so frustrating. *If only you knew, Lisa.* Having a steady boyfriend was not as simple as some girls thought. Especially if that boy was Steve. He could seem so cavalier, so nonchalant about some things. It took every ounce of Katie's patience to stay calm in matters like this. The discussion in the next room faded as the three girls exited the art room. Katie sighed. She would just have to phone Steve tonight and come right out and bring up the topic of the banquet.

Friday night when Steve picked Katie up for the banquet, Mrs. Fremont took some pictures of them in front of the Christmas tree. Steve, looking slightly uncomfortable dressed in a tie and suit coat, went along with it good-naturedly and told Katie's mother he was sure his mom would want a picture, too. Covertly, under the eyes of her parents, Steve took in every detail of Katie's appearance. She was wearing a long, gauzy dress of pale lavender and her hair was done up with curls cascading down around her shoulders. He got up his nerve and asked Katie's mom if she would take a picture just of Katie. He would cherish a photograph of Katie looking as she did for this evening.

As soon as possible, he ushered Katie out to his truck. The December evening was chilly and the clouds seemed heavy with a promise of rain or snow. Steve had kept his truck running, with the heater going. Katie was grateful for the heat, as she had only worn a light-gray cardigan sweater over her dress. Steve shut the passenger door behind Katie and went around the truck to climb into his side. Before fastening his seatbelt, he turned on the bench and reached for Katie's hand.

"I'll be the envy of all the other guys tonight. You look beautiful, Katie." He let the compliment settle on her, before he continued, "Will you forgive me? I don't want to spend the evening wondering if I'm in the doghouse with you. I can't believe I let you go a whole week wondering about the two of us going together tonight." He rubbed his thumb across the back of her hand. "It was so obvious in my mind, I guess I just didn't realize that I still needed to ask you. It was wrong of me to take that, and you, for granted. I'm sorry."

Katie smiled. When Steve looked at her that way, with a light shining through those brilliant eyes and a boyish expression on his face, she felt she could forgive him for anything. She wanted to reach up and muss his hair, but since they were headed out to a fancy dinner, she kept her hands on her lap. "I forgive you," she simply stated.

"You're so good to me." Steve opened his glove box and drew out a small box wrapped in Christmas paper. "I want to give you your present early. I feel like a little kid at Christmas and can't wait to watch you open it. Besides, I thought if you were still a little mad at me, it might smooth the waters. I'd be proud if you would wear it tonight."

He handed the box to Katie and watched expectantly as she carefully unwrapped it. Laying the paper on the seat between them, Katie fingered the long, slender jeweler's box. Glancing at him first, she slowly lifted the lid. Inside, on a strip of cotton was a silver chain with a locket at the end. "Oh, Steve," she breathed deeply, and gently lifted the necklace out of the box. "It's beautiful." The locket was on a long-enough chain that Katie could slip it over her head without needing to undo the clasp. After putting it on, she held the locket out and looked down at it. "You are so sweet. Thank you. I love it. I'll be delighted to wear this not just tonight but always."

Steve reached an arm around Katie's neck and gently pulled her close. He gave her a brief, tender kiss on her mouth. "I hope this locket will always remind you that we belong together. I believe it, Katie. Do you?"

She nodded her head. Why had she ever doubted him? This dating business was new to both of them. There were bound to be some rocky spots along the way. Katie looked at Steve's hand, holding hers. As always, she felt secure with her hand in his larger one. She gave his hand a squeeze, and then looking into his blue eyes, she said softly, "I believe it, too."

Chapter 10

DECISIONS

It was the end of January. For the high school seniors, the calendar pages were flipping too quickly. The time to make decisions that would alter the course of their lives was drawing closer. Soon after the soccer team had gone to the state tournament, Steve began to receive calls and letters from colleges offering him soccer scholarships. The material he was collecting made a pile on his bedroom desk. The choices and possibilities excited him, but at the same time, they overwhelmed him.

One Saturday afternoon Steve sat at his desk looking over the offers from colleges. He was attempting to sort them into *yes*, *no*, and *maybe* piles. He raked his fingers through his hair in frustration as he realized the *maybe* pile was by far the deepest. *I'm not making much progress here, Lord,* he breathed. *Where would you have me go?* Steve's thoughts turned to Wayne and Katie. They had gone to a college fair with Diana that day. They hadn't told him straight out, but he knew Wayne and Katie were waiting on his decision before they made their own.

Wayne had been by Steve's side almost constantly for the past ten years. For Steve, his relationship with Wayne had always been one of best friends, even before they were brothers. Becoming Wayne's brother had cemented their relationship and Steve would not trade those years for anything. However, at this point in his life, Steve was willing to move on, and if it meant moving away, he could handle it. But he was concerned for his brother. Wayne had always been very dependent on him. He did not think Wayne was ready for a full-scale separation. Partially for that reason, Steve felt compelled to think about colleges that were within a few hours drive from home.

His thoughts turned to Katie. He thought about her vibrant green eyes, the long blond hair, her sweetness, her patience and her love for people. *She still makes my hair stand on end.* He knew that he loved her. He had not said the words to her yet…they seemed too sacred…but deep in his heart he knew it. He had only known her a few months, but he knew he wanted to spend the rest of his life loving her. Steve knew that Katie had dreams, too. She wanted to be a nurse and he was sure she would be a good one. She had talked about living at home and beginning work on her degree at the community college. She had expressed her need for stability. With the upheaval of her family's recent move, he could understand why she did not want to go far away to attend college.

Steve absentmindedly picked up a pencil and tapped it on the desk. He knew from Wayne, who knew from Diana that what Katie really wanted was to be a mom. To be a wife and a mother. *Father,* Steve prayed, *you gave Katie all the gentleness there is in life. She will make the best nurse, the best wife, the best mother.* Steve felt his blood warming at the thought of Katie being a wife and a mother. His wife. They were just so young and they had a lot of schooling ahead of them—years of it, in fact. Momentarily, a heaviness weighed down on Steve as he thought of all that lay ahead of him and the fulfillment of his dreams and goals. He bowed his head and breathed a simple prayer. *Please help make my way clear, Lord.*

Going to school and playing soccer should not need to take him too far away from his beloved Katie or his brother. Having reached a decision, he sorted through the college papers until he found the one he was looking for. He laid it aside and swiped all the rest into the wastebasket. The one he saved was for a small Christian college in northern Oregon. It was only two hours from home. He could pursue his academic and athletic dreams, but still be close enough to come home for weekend visits.

Steve felt as if a load of bricks had been lifted from his shoulders. Katie could stay here and go to the community college if that's what she really wished. His thoughts scattered, as there was a rushed knock on his door. Wayne, Katie and Diana breezed in, bringing with them the smell of rain.

"Hey," Steve greeted them, "how was it?"

"I've made a decision!" Diana announced, twirling around.

Wayne chuckled. "She goes to a college fair and decides not to go to college."

"So what are you going to do?" Steve asked, genuinely interested.

"Wayne's right. It suddenly dawned on me today that I don't fit that college scene. You know, I'm not the greatest student. I don't crave knowledge, so..." with her own unique flair, Diana made her announcement, "I'm going to work at a bank. When I start earning enough money, I'll even get my own apartment. I feel so relieved that I don't have to keep on with school."

Steve chuckled. Everything was so easy for Diana. Here he had been struggling for weeks with his decision and she naively goes to a college fair and arrives home a few hours later with her mind made up. "Good for you, Diana," Steve gave her a high five. Then he looked at Wayne and Katie. "And you two?"

Wayne threw himself down on Steve's bed. "I'm more confused than ever. Now I'm thinking, why don't I combine school with travel? You know, I could go to the University of Hawaii." Wayne looked hopefully up at Steve. "You wouldn't want to go there, would you?"

Steve laughed again. "I play soccer, Wayne, I don't surf. Actually," Steve paused and held out a hand to Katie. He gently pulled her over next to his chair. "I've made up my mind, too. There must be something in the air today, Diana."

Katie closed her eyes and held her breath. *Please, Lord, don't take him too far away.*

Wayne sat up. "Okay. So which school is getting a new soccer goalie?"

Steve held up the school catalog for them all to see. "Pacific Christian College."

"All right!" Wayne nodded. "That's not too far away. I can deal with that. *We* can deal with that, can't we, Katie?"

Katie let out her breath. *Thank you, Lord.* "Yes," she said to Wayne. She faced Steve and searched his eyes. "Is this really what you want?"

"God and I made the decision together, Katie." His love for her radiated from his eyes. "I won't be too far away."

Chapter 11

SOCCER, WAYNE, KATIE

On a late Monday afternoon in early April, Katie sat on her family's porch swing. Purple crocuses and bright yellow daffodils dancing in the breeze, lined the front walk. Katie, wearing jeans and a light yellow sweatshirt, sat wrapped in an old army blanket. One leg dangled over the swing so she could gently push herself while she read a novel from the school library.

At the sound of footsteps, she looked up to see Steve approaching the porch. He was dressed in his warm-ups and carried a brown grocery bag. "Hi," he greeted.

Katie's face lit up with pleasure at the unexpected visit. "Steve! I didn't think I would see you tonight. What's in the bag?"

"Soup bones, I guess. From my mom to yours. I'll bring them inside a minute. Don't get up, I'll be right back."

Katie settled back and read a few more paragraphs before Steve returned through the front door. "I couldn't find anyone home so I just put them in the freezer."

"Mom took Rachel to piano lessons. Dad's at church."

"That means you're home alone," Steve said pleasantly as he slid down onto the seat next to her.

Katie closed her book and laid it on the porch railing. Steve took her hand and laced his fingers with hers. "I can't stay too long. I've got a game tonight."

"I know," Katie replied. "I'm sorry I can't come tonight. I've got to finish this book for my book report, plus I have a test in math tomorrow."

"That's okay." Relaxing, Steve slouched in the swing and laid his head back. "Wayne will be there."

"Tonight is your last game for indoor soccer, isn't it?"

"Yep. Thursday we start practice for spring league."

Katie stiffened. "There's spring league?"

"You bet. It'll be so great to get outside after playing indoors all winter."

"And you have to do this? Play spring league too? Is there no end to soccer?"

Steve sat up and studied Katie's face. "Katie, I'm going to college on a soccer scholarship. I have to play year round to stay in shape and keep sharp."

"Oh," Katie sighed and picked at the blanket with her free hand. "I had just hoped you would have more free time after tonight."

Steve gave Katie a brief kiss on her forehead. "I'm sorry, Katie, but soccer will be a big thing for the next four years. I hope you're in it for the long haul with me."

Katie nodded, but did not say anything. Thinking the topic settled, Steve shifted gears. "Guess what? Wayne did a call-in thing at KWGN and won two tickets to a concert for Saturday night. Cool, huh? He wants me to go with him. Thing is, it's in Tacoma so we'll need to leave about four o'clock or so and won't get home until midnight or later. I guess I won't be able to go out this weekend, sorry."

"Is there something going on Friday that I don't know about?" Katie bristled, her voice rising slightly.

"Didn't I tell you? After practice, Wayne and I are going to pull the truck engine apart. I've got to find that oil leak." Steve checked Katie's face. He could tell she was not happy. "It's the only time I have for it, Katie," he reasoned.

Katie pulled her hand away from Steve's. "And let me just clarify this," she said. "Is next weekend when you, Wayne and John have to help with the boys' club at your church?"

Steve did some calculating in his head. "Hey, yeah. That is next weekend."

Now in a huff, Katie struggled out from under the army blanket.

"I can't believe you would do this. To me. To us. I can't believe that after all this time I mean so little to you!"

Steve looked bewildered. "I don't know what you're talking about."

Too angry to continue sitting, Katie stood up and faced him. "Then let me clue you in! Too many weekends go by like this. You have time for everything but me."

"That's not fair, Katie. Just Saturday we went out for pizza."

"Yes, but after your game and with half of your teammates."

"I thought you had fun," Steve countered, confused by Katie's anger.

"That's not the point." Katie felt the tears rising. "It's obvious that I'm not high enough on your priority list, Steve Anderson. You don't have enough time for me."

Steve tried to hold his anger in check. "Think back to the beginning, Katie. I warned you about that right up front. Remember, I told you about how busy I am. After that first week of school, I offered to walk away from this relationship. If you had wanted me to do that, I would have chosen to leave then, before we invested all this—this—."

"This what, Steve? Were you going to say TIME?" Katie tossed out sarcastically.

Exasperated, Steve raked a hand through his hair. He bit his tongue to keep from lashing out at Katie. She stamped her foot in an effort to hold back her tears.

"Katie, you can't deny we had the conversation."

"That was a long time ago. I thought it wouldn't matter to me. I didn't know that soccer would go on all year. That it would rule your life." Katie turned away from him as the tears began to trickle down her cheeks. "You're my knight in shining armor. I thought you were perfect." Katie turned back toward him and nearly spit her next words at him. "I didn't know that what you really are is egotistical and selfish."

Steve stood up and faced her, holding his hands out in front of him. "Oh, come on, Katie. Nobody's perfect. You shouldn't have put me on a pedestal."

Katie wiped her nose with the cuff of her sweatshirt. "It's soccer and Wayne, soccer and Wayne. I'm tired of competing. I feel like I always come out on the losing side."

"It's not a competition, Katie, it's just my life. I have a lot of things going on and there are three things that are most important to me. Maybe, for some people, it's easier and they can focus on just one thing." He stopped talking to study her face.

"Go on," she crossed her arms and waited. "Your three things being…?"

"Isn't it obvious to you?" He held out his fingers one at a time as he counted them off. "Soccer, Wayne, you."

Katie glared at him. She could hardly believe what she had just heard Steve say. "In *that* order?"

"Huh? No, there's no order."

"You named me last, Steve Anderson! Whether you thought about it or not, that's what you did. Is it always going to be Wayne before me?"

"Katie," Steve's voice became low and measured, "Wayne has been like a part of me for ten years. Don't make me choose between the two of you." Steve began to pace a small section of the porch. "Don't make me do it, Katie."

"Fine!" Katie reached around her neck and pulled the locket that Steve had given her for Christmas up over her head. "I won't ask you. I'll do it for you. You just chose Wayne." Sobbing, Katie flung the necklace at Steve and ran into the house, letting the door slam behind her.

Steve looked from the tangled necklace in his hand to the house door and back again. *What just happened here?* He took a step or two toward the front door, and then in a daze, walked down the sidewalk to his truck. Dismally, he climbed onto the seat and hung Katie's necklace from the rearview mirror. He stared at it for a moment, then fingered the heart pendant and gave it a push so it began to swing. Steve started the engine and, in a state of bewilderment, slowly drove away.

A few hours later, Wayne bounded up the stairs in his house and thrust open the door to Steve's bedroom. He found his brother sprawled on his back on his bed, staring up at the ceiling. "Where have you been?" Wayne demanded. "I went to your game, but you never showed. They had to put John in as keeper." Wayne waited for a response. When one did not come, he tried again. "Did you hear what I said? It was your last game. They had to play John in your spot. Where were you? Are you sick?"

Steve put an arm over his face. "I was driving around." His voice came out muffled.

"You were driving around? Then you're not sick?"

"We had a fight."

"Who?" Wayne felt behind him for the desk chair and eased himself into it.

"Me and Katie."

"What happened?"

"I'm not sure." Steve rubbed his hand over his forehead.

Wayne felt a lump growing in his throat. "Did you hurt her?"

"I don't know. I tried not to. I sure didn't mean to if I did. She gave this back to me." Steve held out an arm. Katie's chain dangled from his palm.

Wayne reached out and grasped it. "Oh, man, what did you guys fight about?"

Steve rolled over and faced the wall. "I don't want to talk about it, Wayne. Just leave me alone."

The next morning it was raining. Diana arrived at school early and staked out the parking lot waiting for Wayne to arrive. Almost as soon as he had parked his car, she was standing beside his door. "What are we going to do?" she asked firmly.

"I don't know, Di," Wayne slowly slung his backpack over his shoulders and shut his car door. "I'm clueless here. What did Katie say? What did they fight about?"

"I don't know." Diana fell in step beside Wayne as they walked toward the high school building. "She was crying so hard over the phone she could barely talk. About all I could make out was that it's over."

Wayne stopped walking and faced Diana. "She broke his heart, Diane," he said, accusingly. "She gave him the Christmas locket back."

"Oh my! I didn't know that. She's so upset. I suppose he is too."

"That's an understatement." Wayne kicked a pebble across the parking lot in his frustration. "I told you we would be left to pick up the pieces. I did tell you that, didn't I?"

"But what can we do now?"

"I don't know. Let's see how the day progresses. Maybe it will all blow over. In a school this small, they can't exactly ignore each other."

However, that is just what Steve and Katie did. They managed to stay on opposite sides of the room whenever they had a class together. They averted their eyes in the hallway. The tension between the pair soon spread through the entire senior class. By lunch break, it seemed as if the whole school knew about the break-up. Classmates speculated on the reason, but no one knew anything for certain. A depression settled over some of the girls who had seen Steve and Katie as 'the class couple.'

Through it all, Ryan looked smug. He had figured that someone like Steve would not know how to keep a girl. Ryan understood women, or so he thought. After all, he had dated around a lot, ever since his sophomore year. Steve had only taken a couple of girls out, once or maybe twice. After gym class, Ryan accosted Wayne at the drinking fountain. "No hope for me, eh? We'll just see about that."

Wayne balled his hand in a fist and had to restrain himself from throwing Ryan up against the lockers. "Scum bag," he muttered.

That night at the supper table Steve just pushed his food around on his plate. "May I be excused, Mom?" he finally asked.

His mother started to protest, but Wayne said quietly, "Let him go, Mom."

As Steve rose and left the room, David quickly reached his arm across the table to grab his brother's plate. "Can I have his chicken?"

"What's wrong with your brother?" Mr. Anderson asked, buttering a roll.

"He and Katie broke up last night."

"Oh, that poor girl," Mrs. Anderson put a hand to her breast.

"Poor girl?" Wayne croaked, staring at his mother. "What about Steve, Mom? She broke his heart. She ripped it out of his chest and trampled it in the dirt."

"Gross!" piped up eight-year-old Adam.

"Wayne," his father reprimanded, "that is no way to talk about Katie."

Mrs. Anderson patted Wayne's arm. "Now, dear, I feel sorry for Steve. You know that I do, but there are always two sides to every story. Katie is one of the sweetest, most patient girls I know. Perhaps he did something that broke her heart as well."

"Can I be excused?" Wayne asked.

At Mr. Anderson's nod, Wayne handed his plate to David. "Here, you can have mine too."

Wayne dragged his feet up the steps and leaned against the open door to Steve's room. He stood still and observed Steve as he mindlessly strung paper clips together to form a chain. Katie's locket hung from a knob on the dresser.

"What did you do to her?" Wayne demanded. "What did you say?"

"Nothing. I tried to reason with her." Steve turned around and looked at his brother. "There is no reasoning with girls. Don't get involved, Wayne." Steve turned back to his paper clips and added another one to his chain. "You can't fix this."

Wayne shoved his hands in the pockets of his jeans. "I'm already involved. Did you even think of that? She was my friend too, but now I don't think she'll want much to do with me."

"Yeah, I know," Steve agreed. "You and I are kind of a packaged deal. Sorry."

The next morning Diana again approached Wayne's car as he turned off his engine. "How much longer can this go on, Wayne? Did you learn anymore? Katie won't tell me anything."

"Well," Wayne took a deep breath. "There's one thing I figured out last night. They're still very much in love."

"What? How can you say that?"

"It's simple, Diane. Look at how miserable they are. Steve can't eat, can't sleep. I heard him prowling around half the night. Something's gotta give. Let's give them a little more time."

The two friends stopped walking and watched Katie pull her silver car into a parking spot. Katie had spent the last thirty-six hours in a fog. She had flunked her math test. Her novel still sat on the porch railing. Today she had come to school with no makeup on and her hair was carelessly pulled back with a scarf of her mother's that clashed with the sweater she wore.

"She's an emotional wreck," Diana said.

"Aren't we all?" Wayne muttered.

On Wednesdays, second hour was chapel. The entire school, staff and students, met in the auditorium. A fifteen-minute break always followed chapel so students were free to mill around and talk afterward.

Wearily, Steve climbed to the top of the bleachers and found a seat in the back row. Diana led Katie by the hand to a few open seats in the third row. Wayne was on stage, adjusting the microphones and getting ready to lead the students in worship. He grimaced when he saw Ryan slip into the open seat next to Katie and attempt to engage her in conversation. "Jerk," he mumbled under his breath.

As the lights dimmed and Patti turned on the overhead projector, Wayne picked up his guitar and began playing what he assumed was the opening song for that day's chapel. It was not what the rest of the band had begun playing, nor what was projected on the overhead screen. He stopped playing and tried to cover with a joke, "I don't know what's wrong with my head." The joke fell flat however, because the majority of the upper classmen did know what was wrong with Wayne's head. They all knew he was Steve's brother and that Steve and Katie's problems deeply affected him as well. Even some of the faculty had discussed the situation that morning in the staff room.

Mr. Porter, the principal, had been pouring himself a second cup of coffee when he had commented to a few teachers standing nearby,

"In a school this small, a major break-up like this Anderson-Fremont one affects everybody. I've seen it before."

"Only the freshmen seem oblivious to what's going on," Mrs. DeSmit put in.

"When Katie Fremont fails a math test, you know something is wrong," added Mr. Jennings.

Mr. Larson had promised to talk to both Steve and Katie at some point during the day.

Now, with all eyes on him, Wayne flipped through the music on his stand for the correct song. *Please, Father God,* he silently prayed, *help me turn this around. Even in the midst of this mess, we desire to worship you.* He found the correct sheet music and asked the students to rise and start again. As he played, Wayne closed his eyes and allowed the music to envelope him and fill him with peace as music had always done for him. Just for these moments, while he played for chapel, he could forget about Steve...and Katie...and center his thoughts on his Creator, his Savior.

Steve remained seated as the other students around him rose and began to sing. He knew he could not possibly get any sound past his throat, but he did close his eyes and let the music ease his hurting heart. For his heart did hurt. It hurt badly because he loved Katie so much, and because he did not even begin to understand what the problem was. Confusion swirling in his mind, he tried to sort out the issues that Katie had exploded over. He probably should have never let her into his life. *Like I had any choice*, he reasoned with himself. *When a girl gets under your skin like she has...well...there's not much you can do about it.* By the third song, as the mass of voices filled the auditorium, the words to the song they were singing caught his attention and made it past his ears and down to his very soul. The students were singing about how Jesus had borne the sins of each person on his shoulders when he hung on the cross. That it was through his agonizing death that man is brought to eternal life.

As the students went on to sing the next verse, Steve kept hearing one line repeatedly in his mind. That Jesus had died for his sin. *My sin.* A tear ran down Steve's cheek. *Oh God!* He cried out in his heart. *I am a sinner! Too often I don't give you the honor and the glory for my talents. For my soccer skills and my good grades and...I am nothing on my own.* He thought about Katie and his heart wrenched as he recalled their conversation, word by painful word. Suddenly it dawned on him that when he had named for Katie the three things that were the most important in his life, he had not mentioned God. *Oh Father,* another tear slid down Steve's cheek. He leaned his head back against the wall. *I've taken you so for granted. Maybe that's why things are so messed up right now. Please, forgive me.* He felt like a miserable lowlife. Katie's accusations against him were true. *I am what Katie said. I am egotistical and selfish. And, God, I did hurt her. I don't always honor her, either. I'm sorry, Father. I'm sorry.*

 Steve opened his eyes and wiped the tears from his face with the back of his hand. He had to talk to Katie. He had to apologize and set things right. The student body resumed their seats as the speaker for the day climbed the steps to the podium. *I have to talk to Katie!* Steve wiggled in his seat as he tried to find her in the sea of bodies before him. Then he spotted her. Down near the front, she was sitting between Diana and Ryan. *Ryan!* A flame of jealousy ripped through Steve's gut. "I have to talk to Katie," he said aloud to John, who sat next to him. "I have to talk to Katie now!"

 "You'll have to wait," John whispered. "Be quiet and sit still."

 Somehow, Steve made it through to the end of chapel. The speaker's words just washed over him. As quickly as he could, he made it down from the top row of seats. "I have to talk to Katie," he kept muttering under his breath. He looked around, but could not find her. Jumping onto the stage, he grabbed Wayne's arm. "Where's Katie?" he hissed.

 Wayne shrugged and continued folding the music stand. His heart soared, though, and he began to scan the crowd of milling students for a sight of Katie.

 Steve grabbed a microphone from its stand and turned it on. "Katie!" His voiced pleaded through the sound system. "Katie Fremont." Suddenly the room was wrapped in silence as every head turned toward the stage. Katie turned from Jessica and Diana at the sound of her name. "Katie, I'm sorry." Steve's apology reverberated throughout the auditorium. Ryan slunk out the side door. Wayne, having spotted Katie, put a hand on Steve's back and pointed to her. Steve thrust the microphone at Wayne, but did not take his eyes off Katie. Her eyes met his across the room and their fellow students backed out of the way.

Whispers flooded the room.

"Who's Katie?" a freshman girl asked.

"That's embarrassing," came from a sophomore boy.

"True romance is alive and well," voiced a girl from the senior class.

Oblivious to all the whispering and commotion starting up around them, Steve and Katie met each other halfway.

"Katie," Steve's legs felt almost too weak to hold him up, "can you ever forgive me? I've been so wrong."

"Don't apologize, it's all my fault," a tear streaked down Katie's face. "I called you such terrible names."

Steve put his hands on her shoulders. "Look at me, Katie. You were right. I was being a jerk. I didn't think. I never looked at things from your perspective."

"Hush," Katie whispered. "We'll work it out. I want to work it out."

Steve wrapped Katie in his arms. It did not matter to him that nearly a hundred students were still in the room, many of them watching this scene unfold before them. He looked deeply into Katie's green eyes and for the first time he said, "I love you, Katie."

Katie studied the face that was so dear to her. "Without a doubt, I love you, too."

They hugged for a moment longer, then Katie said, "You didn't tell Wayne about my tirade, did you? You didn't tell him that I demanded you choose him over me?"

"Never." With a tender touch, Steve wiped a tear from Katie's cheek. "Never." He pulled her to him for one more embrace. "I will never break trust with you," he promised.

Taking a step back, he drank in the sight of Katie. His eyes moved from her face to her hair and he chuckled. "What's this?" Gently he tugged the gaudy scarf off her head. "Here." He fished in the pocket of his blue jeans for her locket which he had been carrying around for two days. "This will look much better on you than that old scarf," he said as he tenderly placed the chain around her neck. "This is for always, remember?"

Katie, tears still glistening in her eyes, nodded her head and she grasped the pendant in her hand. "I remember."

Chapter 12

I WILL BE THERE

Katie sat at the kitchen table with her sister, Rachel, eating their dad's famous Saturday morning waffles. Her mother had remained in bed with a headache. It had been a week and a half since she and Steve had made up following their fight. The locket he had given her swung from her neck. As Katie poured blueberry syrup on her second waffle, the doorbell rang.

"I'll get it," Rachel offered. She jumped up, and pushed her syrup-laden plate away. "I'm finished anyway." She padded toward the front door in her slippers and blue nightgown.

A few moments later, Wayne peeked around the kitchen entryway. He took in the sight of Katie at the table wearing her jeans and a USA t-shirt, barefoot, with her hair in a loose ponytail. He glanced at her dad who stood at the waffle maker, turning a waffle and sipping coffee at the same time.

"'Morning, Pastor Fremont. Hi Katie."

"Wayne!" Surprised, Katie greeted him.

Katie's dad eyed him over the rim of his large black coffee cup. "Can you use some breakfast, Son?"

"Well," Wayne looked at the waffle on Katie's plate. "I did eat once, but that looks pretty good. I won't say no."

Pastor Fremont laid a plate-sized waffle across the table from his daughter. "Katie, get him some silverware and juice," he said as he picked up Rachel's dirty dishes.

While Katie got the items for Wayne, he slipped out of his black, zippered, hooded sweatshirt and straddled the chair. Accepting the knife from Katie, he topped his waffle with a mound of butter and poured syrup on it.

Katie sat back down across the table from him and, in sheer amazement, watched Wayne eat. "And you say this is your second breakfast? What did you have for your first one?"

Wayne shrugged while he hooked another bite onto his fork. "I dunno. Eggs, toast, a Pop-Tart."

Katie took another bite of her own breakfast. It felt so comfortable, so right, to be sitting across from Wayne, sharing breakfast with him.

Wayne lifted up his empty plate. "Hey, Pastor Fremont, you got any more of those? They're really good."

With a flourish, Katie's dad placed another waffle on Wayne's plate. Wayne poured syrup over the top and continued to eat with relish. Around bites of food he said to Katie, "Steve's been holding out on me. He never told me that your dad makes killer waffles."

In fact, Steve had never been to her house for breakfast before, but Katie didn't want to admit that to Wayne. Laying down her fork, she said cheerfully, "What are you doing here, Wayne? Did you open your front door and decide to follow this amazing waffle smell across town?"

"No," Wayne sighed and pushed his plate away. "Man, that was good. Pastor Fremont, do you make these every Saturday? I might be back." He shook his hand at the pastor's offer for more and handed his and Katie's plates to her dad. Turning back to Katie, he said, "I came over, because I want to talk to you before I go to work."

"Work? You got a job?"

"Didn't Steve tell you? I started a couple of weeks ago." He paused to think, then said, "Well, I guess in all the mess of last week he didn't get around to telling you. I'm working at the music store in the mall. It's fun, but it's only a few hours a week."

"Fantastic! That is a perfect job for you."

While Pastor Fremont began loading the dishwasher and cleaning up the kitchen, Wayne wiped his mouth with a napkin. "That's actually not what I came over to tell you. I've got it all figured out, Katie." Enthusiasm filled Wayne's voice. "I'm going to stay here and go to school with you at the community college."

"What?" Katie was surprised. "No University of Hawaii – or Morocco – or..."

She laughed and studied his face. Even with his broad shoulders and rugged good looks, he could look like a little boy sometimes. Moreover, his thick brown hair never stayed in place. Katie wondered if some gel could tame those unruly locks.

Wayne shook his head. "No, they're too far away. I need to stay closer to Steve. I want to be able to catch some of his games. I'll take you with me. Diane can even come along. It's too soon to break up the four musketeers. But that's not all my news. I finally know what I want to do." He winked at Katie. "In between my adventures, that is. You know, when I have to be in the real world earning some money."

"So tell me."

"Teach school," Wayne announced. "I'm going to become a teacher. Fifth, sixth, seventh grade. In there, somewhere. Kids that age need a firm hand, gentle guidance, and a whole lot of fun." Wayne's brown eyes were lit up with excitement. "I can do it, Katie, I'm sure of it. I can't wait to introduce them to the realm of geography. And music. And maybe I can do a little soccer coaching on the side. I know I haven't played since sixth grade, but I understand the game inside and out."

"Oh, Wayne," Katie reached a hand across the table to take one of his, and then thinking better of it, she quickly put it on her lap. "You will make a fabulous teacher. I think this is a God-revelation."

"And this is the best part," Wayne paused for dramatic effect, "summers free for traveling." He looked over his shoulder at Katie's dad filling the coffeepot with soapy water. Leaning over the table, he said softly, "Walk me out, Katie, okay?"

She nodded and slid off her chair. Wayne picked up his sweatshirt. "Thanks for breakfast, Pastor Fremont," he said as he led Katie out.

"If you ever get tired of preaching, you could open a waffle house."

Katie's dad chuckled. "I'll keep that in mind, Son."

Wayne held the front door open and whispered to Katie as he ushered her out, "I like it when your dad calls me 'son'." Closing the door behind them, he motioned to the porch swing.

Katie stopped short and stared at the swing. She had not sat there since the afternoon she had said such terrible things to Steve. She did not want to sit there again until Steve was with her. "Let's sit on the steps," she suggested.

"Whatever," Wayne laid his sweatshirt down on the top step and offered the seat to Katie. He settled in next to her and leaned forward with his elbows on his knees. "Listen, Katie, I don't know what went on last week between you and Steve and I don't want to know, but it really shook me up. To be honest, I'm not over it yet. I think you and Steve are moving on, but I'm having trouble here."

"It shook me up, too."

"Well, it shook us all. Diane was breathing down my neck. Steve was inconsolable."

"You can blame me if you want," Katie felt the tears rising in her eyes. "It was all my fault."

Wayne looked at her sharply. "I'm not looking to blame anybody. I don't care whose fault it was. Steve has been loyal to me my whole life, and now he's loyal to you too. You never have to worry about him breaking trust with you and airing your dirty laundry with me. I'm not here to get to the bottom of what happened."

"But you said you're not over it yet."

Wayne looked across the yard at a neighbor's cherry tree that was just beginning to break out in blossoms. "That's because I was scared, Katie. I realized that if Steve loses you, then I do, too. I realized that I don't have any control over my friendship with you because it's all tied up with Steve. I don't want to live with this feeling. It's not that I think you and Steve will break up again, because I don't. I used to think that love at first sight was a bunch of hogwash, but ever since last summer at the Dairy Shack I know that love at first sight is not just a thing in fairy tales." Wayne paused. "It happens.

I've known all along that you and Steve share something special. But, Katie," Wayne turned and locked his gaze with Katie's before continuing. "I want to be your friend on my own account. I need to know that if you and Steve ever do break up or grow apart that you and I can remain friends."

Katie pulled her gaze away from Wayne's intense brown eyes. "I'd like that, too. I like you, Wayne."

"I don't know how we would do it, but we would." Wayne rubbed his hands across his thighs. "Man, last week was bad, Katie. Last summer, at Whisper Lake, Diane and I made a pact that we would keep the four musketeers alive. One for all and all that. We agreed to be there to pick up the pieces if you and Steve ever broke up. Then last week, she and I understood how helpless we really are." Wayne gently turned Katie's chin to face him. "I want to promise you now that no matter what, I will always be there for you. I'll do anything you want, be anything you need. Next year, when Steve is gone, I'll look out for you. I want you to come to me if you ever need anything, okay? Do you get that?"

A tear escaped from Katie's eye and rolled slowly down her cheek. "Do you want to be like a big brother to me?" she asked.

"If that's what you want, Katie. Yes, I'd like that, because families are forever." Wayne put an arm around Katie's shoulder and squeezed it. "Okay," he said, standing up. "That's enough serious talk for now. That was about a year's worth for me."

Katie grinned and wiped her eyes with the back of her hand. She stood up and handed Wayne his sweatshirt. He pulled it on as he said, "I've got to get to work because I'm opening the store this morning. Thanks for listening, Katie."

She watched as Wayne walked to his car. He opened the door and turned to wave, a huge grin on his face. "Have a good day, Sis." He started the engine and pulled out onto the road.

Chapter 13

LIKE A SEAL OVER YOUR HEART

"How about this one?" Stepping away from the department store's display rack, Katie held up a skirt for Diana's approval. The skirt was mid-length, navy with a small yellow and pink floral print.

"Good! That will look nice with this," Diana held up the pale pink cardigan that was draped over her arm. Reaching for the skirt she said, "I better go start trying things on."

"We sure found some cute things. I hope some of them work," Katie said, trailing behind her cousin to the dressing room area.

Diana shot a gleeful look over her shoulder, "Yeah, like all of them! Good thing my dad offered to help me out." Diana patted the wad of money in her pocket. "I'm going to be in here awhile," she said as she opened the door to her dressing room. "If you want to step across and say hi to Wayne, that would be okay. I'll meet you over there when I'm done."

"Okay." Katie wound her way through the cosmetic counters, past the shoe department and entered the mall hallway. Taking a moment to get her bearings, she turned right and headed down the corridor to the music store where Wayne worked.

It was a Saturday, near the end of June. School had been out for two weeks. Wayne's hours at Glenn's Rhythm 'n Blues had increased to full time. Katie entered the store and found him in a back corner restringing a guitar.

"Got time for a cappuccino?" Katie greeted him.

Startled, Wayne looked up from his work. A cheerful smile

replaced the look of concentration on his face. "Katie! Sorry, I've already had my break. If I had known I was going to get an invitation from a pretty girl, I would have waited. What are you doing here?"

"Oh, I've been helping Diana. She started working at a bank a couple days ago. She found out that she can't wear jeans and t-shirts so she needs to do a major upgrade on her wardrobe."

Wayne cocked an eyebrow. "I see, from Denim Di to Posh Princess overnight. Say, are you still looking for a job?" At Katie's nod, he continued, "The card shop two doors down is looking for someone part-time. Maybe you want to check it out."

Katie clapped her hands. "Excellent! I'll go over right now and pick up an application." Turning to leave she said over her shoulder, "If Di beats me back here, restrain her. I want to go to The Gap with her."

A half-hour later, Katie walked back into Rhythm 'n Blues, her face glowing. She marched right up to Wayne who was now unpacking guitar straps from a box. "Wayne Anderson," she announced, "I could kiss you."

Wayne looked around the store. His boss and two customers had overheard the remark and were looking over at the pair. Wayne smiled and spread out his arms. "Another satisfied customer!" he declared loudly. To Katie he whispered, "And what's to stop you?"

Katie paused, and then gave Wayne a peck on the cheek. "It's amazing! I talked to Gina, the manager. She's really nice, but she must be desperate. I got the job and I can start on Monday."

"Way to go," Wayne gave Katie a high five. "Aw, here comes the princess," he said, looking over Katie's shoulder.

Diana, laden with two large shopping bags greeted them. "Not only do these new clothes make me look sophisticated, they also make me look older. Twenty-something. I decided that might be helpful in attracting a guy."

"You don't need any help, you goof."

Diana gave Katie a stern look. "Okay, Miss Going-Steady-With-Steve, which one of us did not have a date to the senior banquet?" Diana waved off Katie's attempt to reply. "I figured out something else, too. As a bank teller, I can probably find out how much money a guy has in his checking account. When I find a rich one, I'll just set a trap for him."

Wayne's chin dropped as he looked from Diana to Katie. "Is she serious?"

The girls laughed. "Guys!" Diana teased. "They're so simple-minded. Come on, Katie, I still have some of Dad's money. Let's go to The Gap."

Wayne eyed the bulging sacks that Diana held. "Isn't that enough?"

Diana batted her eyelashes at him. "Shopping for girls is kind of like eating for guys. There's never an end."

"Remind me not to get married," Wayne muttered. "I could never afford it."

The girls waved goodbye and as they turned to leave, Katie began to tell Diana about her new job. Katie was excited about it, but she did wonder if this would make it even more difficult to find time to be with Steve. He had returned to his job at his dad's office downtown and had also moved from playing spring league to summer soccer.

As the Fourth of July approached, their friend, Lisa, planned a beach party at her parents' cabin on Blue Lake. The cabin was situated on lake front property with a sandy beach and a long dock. The lake was ideal for swimming and skiing. Traditionally at dusk on Independence Day, the county set off a large display of fireworks from a barge in the middle of the lake.

Lisa's father had given permission for Lisa to host a Twelve-for-Twelve party: twelve kids from twelve noon to twelve midnight. Her guest list included Diana, Katie, Wayne, Steve, Jessica, Tami, Tami's new boyfriend, Jeff, John, Ryan, Mike and Tracy.

A few days before Lisa's party, Katie sat cross-legged on the ground watching one of Steve's evening soccer games. It was a rare event for Wayne not be watching with her, but it was his night to close up the store. Mr. and Mrs. Anderson and David were sharing Katie's blanket. Steve's youngest brother, Adam, was dribbling a soccer ball with his feet as he ran in circles behind them.

"Katie," he called, "when I'm as old as Steve, I'm going to play in the pro's."

Katie looked back at him and smiled in encouragement. The referee blew his whistle, which signified the end of the game. Steve's team had won, 2 to 1. There were cheers and high fives on the field as the team lined up to shake hands with the opposing players.

"It was such a nice evening for a game," Mrs. Anderson commented as her husband helped her to her feet. "David, Adam, gather up your things." Turning to Katie, she smiled warmly and said good night.

Katie hung back while Steve's family met him as he came off the field. His mom handed him a sport drink and his dad shook his hand. David and Adam had raced ahead to the car, so after the brief exchange with his parents, Steve was free to join Katie. He lowered himself to the blanket, took off his cleats and shin guards and stretched his legs out in front of him.

"You looked good out there," Katie complimented.

Steve reached over and ran a finger across her cheek. "You look good right here. You always look good."

"You could turn a girl's head with your sweet talk."

"Not just any girl, though." He fingered some of the long blond strands of Katie's hair. "Just yours. You know, having a girlfriend was never part of my plan, Katie." He intertwined his fingers with hers. "I've had dreams and goals for my life and I never once envisioned a special girl being part of. At least not for another six years or so. I guess God knew how badly I needed someone like you." Steve grinned, his dimples showing, and winked at her. "See, when I tell you that you've turned my whole life upside-down, I mean it."

"So I've messed up all your plans, have I?" Katie's green eyes sparkled in merriment. "I realize it hasn't been easy loving me."

"N–o-o-o," Steve drawled, "it hasn't been easy at all!" He began to tickle her stomach. She giggled and rolled away from him, her long hair cascading over her face. Steve brushed it aside and gave her a brief kiss. "I'll just have to figure out what to do with this girl that God gave me."

They sat for a while in companionable silence while the sun moved lower in the western sky, turning the wispy clouds a bright orange. Steve thought about his and Katie's future and what plans they might make. He was not ready to talk with her about it yet, so he brought his thoughts around to present day events. "What time should I pick you up for Lisa's party? Did you get off work?"

"No, but I got the first shift. Gina has little kids and she wanted to have the morning off to take them to the parade. I have to open the store, but I'm off at two."

"Okay, I'll pick you up at the mall then."

"No, don't do that. You go ahead out to Lisa's right away. I'll be there by 3:00. You can get a lot of skiing in. I'm fine, really, with coming later by myself."

Steve sat up. "Are you sure? I don't care if I go late to the party."

"Yes, I'm fine. Wayne's boss gave him the whole day off so you can spend the first three hours with him." Katie's green eyes twinkled. "Then when I get there, I won't feel so guilty if I monopolize your time."

On the morning of Lisa's party, the sky was overcast, but it cleared by late morning. Friends began arriving at the Ross' cabin a little before noon. Everyone except Katie was there by 1:30. Around 2:00, the girls gathered in the kitchen to bake up a couple of pans of brownies.

"My grandma always says the way to a man's heart is through his stomach," Jessica quipped, cracking eggs into a bowl.

"Maybe we should each make a pan," Lisa suggested, "and present it to one of the eligible bachelors out there." She glanced out the window to where the boys were playing a rowdy game of football on the beach.

"Well," Diana said, "only three of us need to bake the brownies then. Tami, Tracy and Katie have already found the way to their guys' hearts."

"It's so easy for some girls," Lisa sighed. "Take Katie. She hadn't even been here for two weeks when she managed to snag the heart of the most dreamed-over guy in our class."

"But she did it without flirting and playing games with him," Diana spoke up for her cousin. "It all happened so naturally."

"I'm not faulting her, Diana," Lisa said. "I think they make a very sweet couple. None of us were making any headway with Mr. Blue Eyes anyway. I'd much rather Katie have him than one of the junior girls."

"I think she's been good for him," Tami added, spreading brownie mix into a pan. "She's smoothed over some of his rough edges."

"Those brownies ready yet?" Ryan's loud voice carried through the open window from the yard.

Jessica laughed. "What did I tell you?" She slid the two pans into the oven and Lisa set the timer.

"I guess their game broke up," Tracy reported from the window. "Looks like Mike and Wayne are setting up the volleyball net in the water. Come on, girls, that's much more our speed than football."

Katie had gotten into the spirit of the day and dressed in patriotic colors for work. She wore her blue jean skirt with a sleeveless red top and a white cardigan sweater. She had pulled her long bangs back in a ponytail and had tied a white ribbon in her hair. She left work that afternoon in a good mood.

It had been slow at the mall, but she and Shelly had managed to keep busy rearranging the display window. Gina had supplied them with some of her children's sand buckets and beach toys. She had even had her husband bring in a 5-gallon bucket of sand they could spread around over a plastic tarp. They laughed while they worked and praised each other's creative ideas. *It really looks great,* Katie thought as she took a last look before heading down the mall and out to the parking lot.

When she neared her car, she could see that someone had stuck a gallon-sized zip lock bag under her window wiper. She could see that it had a red flier inside. *That's funny, they don't usually put fliers in baggies. Especially when the sky is clear.* Katie pulled the bag off her windshield and unlocked her car door. She tossed her purse onto the passenger seat and climbed into the hot, stuffy car. Curiously, she opened the plastic bag and took out the flier. She flipped it over to see that the message was printed with a computer's fancy font. She smiled and her heart warmed as she began to read.

Milady,

Remember I told you I am trying to read the entire Bible this year? Well, last night in my reading I came across something that I want to share with you. It so satisfactorily expresses what I cannot on my own. I found it in the Song of Solomon, chapter 8.

'Place me like a seal over your heart,
like a seal on your arm;
for love is as strong as death,
its jealousy unyielding as the grave.
It burns like blazing fire,
like a mighty flame.
Many waters cannot quench love;
rivers cannot wash it away.'

I will be counting the hours until you arrive at the lake.

Forever,

Steve.

Katie held the paper to her heart. Steve could be the most romantic person when he wanted to be. Whenever she was frustrated at their lack of time together, she needed to remember moments like these. After taking a moment to reread Steve's note, she carefully folded it and put it into her purse. She could not wait to see him.

By the time Katie arrived at the beach house, the volleyball game that the others had been playing had deteriorated into a water fight, with the girls on the losing end. Katie could hear the screams and laughter as she climbed out of her car and walked around to the beach side of the cabin. Her first sight of the group was Lisa, Jessica and Tami ganging up to dunk Ryan. Wayne and Mike were holding Tracy by the wrists and ankles and were about to toss her off the end of the dock.

Katie chuckled and let her eyes scan the waterfront to find Steve. He had been watching for her arrival and was attempting to sneak up on her with a pail of water. She caught sight of him out of the corner of her eye just in time to squeal and throw her backpack at him. Steve dropped the bucket, which sent water splashing everywhere.

"Steve," Katie laughed good-naturedly as she scolded him, "I still have my good clothes on!"

Steve, standing in his Hawaiian printed swim trunks, with a towel draped around his neck looked at her sheepishly. "Will you forgive me if I tell you I missed you?"

"I'll think about it," she said, trying to suppress a smile.

Steve took a step closer to her. "How about if I promise you protection from the rest of these hooligans?"

"All day?" Katie asked coyly.

Steve took the remaining step that separated them and placed his hand on his heart. "On my honor as a knight."

"All right," Katie agreed. "By the way, I found something on my car window when I left work today."

Steve leaned closer to her. "You did?" he whispered, grinning, his blue eyes sparkling.

Katie nodded. "It's the sweetest thing you've ever done. I'll cherish it forever."

Suddenly serious, Steve took his hand off his own heart and gently touched it first to Katie's heart and then let it rest on her arm. "I'm placing myself like a seal over your heart and over your arm," he quoted, looking steadily into her eyes. "I love you." Katie took the hand he had on her arm and laced her fingers through it. Squeezing his hand tightly, she accepted the tender kiss he offered.

"Hey, Lover Boy," John teased his friend as he passed the couple on his way to the cabin. "Mr. Ross is getting the boat ready so we can ski. Katie, you better get your swimsuit on."

The afternoon passed too quickly for the friends as they played in the water. They skied, tubed and kneeboarded behind the boat. They also swam and played more water volleyball. About 6:00, Lisa's dad fired up the grill and served an amazing number of hamburgers and hotdogs. Mrs. Ross brought out an array of salads, chips and sodas.

After supper, the gang squeezed around the kitchen table and played games. Pit and Spoons came out on top as favorites. As the evening hours passed, they wandered away from the table in two's and three's to sit outside and wait for the fireworks. They huddled in small groups on beach chairs or blankets spread on the lawn. The weather had cooled so everyone was now dressed in jeans and shoes, with sweatshirts or jackets on.

Steve took Katie's hand and led her beyond the others to the very end of the dock. He sat at the edge and dangled his legs over the side. His feet hung only inches above the water. Katie lowered herself to sit beside him.

"It's beautiful out here," she said softly. As the setting sun turned the colors of the clouds to pink and orange, the scene was reflected on the calm lake water.

Steve put his arm around Katie's shoulders and pulled her close. "*You're* beautiful." As he spoke, the sound of laughter came to them from Wayne, Diana, and John's circle.

Katie cast a glance behind her. "I'll understand if you want to go sit and talk with some of the others."

"If that's what you want, Katie, then okay, but as far as I'm concerned, we've spent most of the day with our friends. I think the rest of the night belongs to us."

Katie leaned her head against Steve's shoulder. "I've always dreamed of watching Fourth of July fireworks with a boyfriend."

"Then it's a night for dreams to come true."

The couple sat in silence for several minutes as they watched bottle rockets and other fireworks that were set off by neighbors across the lake. Katie smiled as she thought back over the day's activities. "We do have a wonderful group of friends, don't we? Last July my dad told me we were moving here. I thought it was the worst thing that could ever happen to me. I was so mad I didn't talk to my family for almost a week. Except for Diana, I didn't expect to find friends here." Steve's arm tightened around Katie as she continued,

"Now it's only a year and God has blessed me beyond all my imaginings."

"If we open ourselves to His will, that's what He has promised."

"I never dreamed I'd find anyone like you."

"Maybe our love is sweeter, because we didn't go looking for it," Steve suggested quietly.

"Perhaps," Katie sighed. "Diana was so great about introducing me around and sharing her friends with me."

"She loves you, Katie. We all love you."

"Well, I love you." Katie glanced behind her. "And all of them."

"Even Ryan?" Steve teased.

"Well," Katie paused, "I'm trying. He sure was funny on those skis today. When he was trying to ski backwards and stuff."

Steve snorted. "Showin' off. He was just showing off in front of you girls."

The main fireworks display started. Everyone settled down to watch the show. When it was over, Mr. Ross made a fire in their fire pit and his wife brought out hot cocoa and the makings for s'mores.

After stuffing themselves and listening to John tell a scary story, Wayne brought out his guitar. They sang some silly rounds to get warmed up, then moved on to praise and worship songs. All too soon, it was midnight and Mr. Ross doused the fire.

Chapter 14

WHISPER AGAIN

It was a warm August night. Mr. and Mrs. Anderson, David, and Adam were asleep. Wayne and Steve had stayed up to watch "Mission Impossible" on the late show. The family room was wrapped in shadows as the only light came from the flickering television set. Wayne sat sprawled on a black beanbag only a few feet in front of the TV. A bowl of popcorn rested on his stomach and a can of Pepsi was on the floor beside him. Steve sat behind his brother on the couch. He held a half-filled cup of cold coffee in his hands and his eyes stared vacantly at the movie.

"Wayne," Steve's voice was barely louder than the low volume of the TV set, "you know how I have to leave early for college because of soccer practice?"

"Yeah," came Wayne's answer, "don't remind me. I've been trying not to think about it."

"Well, I realize you and Katie don't start for a few weeks yet, but next Saturday is my last one at home. I was thinking of taking Katie to Whisper Lake."

"You mean like last year? That was fun. You want us to ask Diane again, too?"

"Not exactly," Steve hesitated. "I was thinking more of just Katie and me going."

Wayne shot his brother a quick look and set down the bowl of popcorn. "Just you and Katie? Did you forget that you and I have been doing this for six years? Are you and Katie so tight now that you have no room for your friends? For me?"

Steve set his coffee cup on an end table and leaned forward, his elbows on his knees and his arms crossed. "I need a special place." He measured his words carefully. "I'm going to ask her to marry me."

Wayne froze as Steve's words fell around him. Music from "Mission Impossible" was the only sound in the room.

"Did you hear what I said, Wayne?"

"Yes. Does Katie have any idea this is coming?"

"No. We've never talked about getting married, but I think that both of us, deep down, know that's where we're heading."

Wayne remained silent. Steve ran his fingers through his hair. "Is there some reason, Wayne, any reason, that I shouldn't ask her? Is that what you're not saying?"

"No," Wayne pressed the mute button on the TV's remote. "That's where I always figured you guys were headed, too. I just didn't expect it so soon. Man, Steve, you have four years of college ahead. Katie's got three."

"I know. I don't have it all figured out yet. Katie and I will have to talk about it. I know we're young, but I just can't go away to school without making a commitment to her." When Wayne did not respond right away, Steve continued, "I talked to her dad last night. He's concerned about how young we are too, but he gave me his blessing." Steve sighed. "Maybe we'll have a long engagement."

Wayne's response came out so quietly it was nearly swallowed by the night. "Long engagements are hard."

"I know," Steve whispered his agreement. The summer warmth and the stillness of the night enveloped them as they sat thinking of the pledge Steve had made. Earlier that winter, when his relationship became serious with Katie, he had vowed that he would remain pure. Brief hugs, handholding and light kissing that was all he would do with Katie. He had asked Wayne to hold him accountable. "I will never take advantage of her," Steve said.

"You'd better take good care of her," Wayne warned. "You hold her heart in your hands."

Steve looked at his hands. "It's a scary thing to hold. A girl's heart. The thing is, she holds a lot more than my heart. She holds my entire being in her hands. What if she says no?"

Wayne nodded silently, feeling the weight of his brother's vulnerability. "Did you get her a ring?"

"I did." Steve gave a nod. "I can pick it up on Wednesday."

"You need some money?"

"I've got it covered, thanks. I should probably tell you though, I had to deplete my South America trip fund."

Wayne picked up the remote and turned off the television set, casting the room in darkness. He did not answer as he felt the death of a dream settle like dead weight upon him.

"I'm sorry, Wayne," Steve said quietly. "I had to make a choice. You can still go. I want you to go."

Wayne closed his eyes and laid his head back against the beanbag. He thought about Steve, his brother. He thought about Katie, his sister-to-be. For Steve's sake, for his own sake, too, he needed to shake off this melancholy mood. Steve needed his support. "It's okay, Bro," he spoke up in the darkness. "Maybe we'll go the next year. Maybe we'll just take Katie along with us. Maybe you guys can come along for your honeymoon."

The tension in the room began to dissipate. "Now there's an intriguing thought," Steve said. "There's just something wrong with that picture."

"Yeah?" Wayne grinned. "What's that?"

"I don't know why I would want to take my brother and his uncle on my honeymoon."

Wayne climbed out of the beanbag and stood up. "I've heard girls like to do a lot of shopping. Maybe you'll need us along to serve as your personal valets. Hey, wait here," Wayne disappeared into the kitchen, turning on the light as he went. When he returned, he carried two cans of Mountain Dew. Handing one to Steve, he said, "Go for it, Bro. Take her up to Whisper Lake." He pulled the tab on the top of his can. "And don't worry about it. She's going to say yes."

Steve took a drink of his pop. "What makes you so sure?"

Wayne shrugged. "She already asked me months ago if I would be her big brother. Think about it, if I'm her brother, what would that make you?"

Steve broke out in a smile.

Steve and Katie crested the trail that led to Whisper Lake. Katie wiped her forehead with a tissue. "It's hotter than last year," she observed, "and I had forgotten how steep that last little bit of the trail is."

"You weren't carrying a pack last year, either." Steve pulled the small daypack off Katie's shoulders before taking off his larger one. He surveyed their surroundings. He almost forgot from year to year what a beautiful spot this was. The serene lake was surrounded by trees. This year there were no fishermen present, but a dad with two young boys swam a little ways down the beach from where Steve and Katie stood. The boys looked about David and Adam's ages and for a brief moment Steve missed not having Wayne along. Shading his eyes from the sun, he took another look around and watched some ducks land on the water. He thought about the ring hidden away in a side pocket of his pack. This remote and peaceful place would serve his purpose very well. He picked up the two packs and headed down the beach away from the dad and his boys. He set the packs near a fire pit and knelt to open his.

Katie had followed him. "Aren't you going to do your ritualistic little jig?"

Steve looked up at her, his blue eyes dancing. "Are you going to do Wayne's part?" Katie shook her head. "Well, I don't think so then." He handed her the waterproof bag of meat and drinks. "Put this in the fridge, will you?"

Katie took the package and put it in the lake as she remembered the routine from last year. Steve pumped up two air mattresses he had brought along. Katie shook out their beach towels and laid them side-by-side near the water's edge.

Steve and Katie shared an enjoyable afternoon. They spent nearly two hours in the lake. They swam, floated on the mattresses, played

Frisbee in knee-deep water and had numerous water fights. Tiring from the horseplay, Katie told Steve she just wanted to sit and relax for a while. He followed her out of the water and pulled on a t-shirt.

"Relaxing sounds good."

After Katie donned shorts and a shirt, she pulled their paperback books from her pack. Laying on their stomachs on the towels, they propped their books in front of them. Katie was soon immersed in her reading of *Gone with the Wind*. Steve's John Grisham's book lay open to chapter ten, but he found he could not concentrate. He had taken care of every detail to make sure everything for this day would work out perfectly. He had even humbled himself and talked to Gina at the card shop. He had needed to explain to Katie's manager why it was so important to give Katie the day off. Now they were here, with perfect weather, Katie looking so beautiful and the ring burning a hole in his backpack. There was only one problem. He had not figured out what he was going to say or how and when to do it.

"I notice you haven't turned a page in your book in a long time." Katie's voice startled Steve out of his reverie. "Is something wrong? Something on your mind?"

"No," Steve closed his book, rolled over and sat up. "Nothing's wrong. I'm fine."

"Okay," Katie said slowly, not sure if she should probe deeper.

"I've just been thinking." Steve cast his eyes around the lake. "I've been listening, too. Do you know why this is called Whisper Lake?"

Katie closed her book and shook her head.

"It's because of a legend they tell around here," Steve began to explain. "Local legend says that if you sit very quietly, you can hear the wind whispering." He paused and sat in silence for a moment. "Can you hear it, Katie? Can you hear the wind whispering?"

Katie rolled over and sat up. She cocked an ear as she looked around the lake. It was very peaceful. The man and his sons had left earlier. The only sounds Katie heard were birds twittering, the buzz of insects, and a slight rustle of the breeze in the trees.

"I hear the wind moving in the leaves," she answered.

Steve looked at the large tree branches over their heads. "Can you hear what it's saying? The wind is whispering your name." Still looking overhead, Steve lowered his voice to a whisper. "Katie – Katie."

Katie smiled, liking the husky sound of Steve whispering her name. "You are terribly sweet and a hopeless romantic."

"I hope I'm not hopeless," Steve said, turning to Katie, "because the wind is whispering something else too. Can you hear it, Katie? It's saying: 'Katie – Katie – marry me – marry me.'"

Katie felt like her body must be going into shock. She turned to look Steve in the eye and found his piercing blue eyes looking deeply into hers. Reaching across the sand, he took her hand in his and held it firmly. "I love you, Katie Fremont. I plan to spend the rest of my life loving you." His voice dropped to a whisper again. "Will you marry me?"

Knowing he waited breathlessly for her answer, Katie nodded her head. She felt like she could not get any words past her throat.

Acknowledging her nod, Steve smiled in relief. "Have I stunned you?"

Katie nodded again, then found her voice. "Yes, and no," she said. "I've felt for a long time that someday you would ask me to marry you. I just didn't expect it today."

"Sit tight," Steve said. He crawled the three or so feet over to his backpack. He dug into the pocket and pulled out the little black velvet box that held Katie's engagement ring. Coming back to Katie, Steve knelt in the sand before her. "Milady," he said, opening the box. The diamond solitaire sparkled in the sunlight.

Tears filled Katie's eyes. At that moment, she realized that Steve had been planning this for some time and that he had not just succumbed to the romance of this place. There was indeed a reason why they had come up here by themselves. She pulled her eyes from the ring to his face and hoped that he could see all the love she felt for him reflected there. "Can you hear what the wind is whispering now, Steve?"

He smiled at her and waited for her to tell him. "Actually," Katie continued, "it's not whispering anymore. It's shouting." Katie raised her voice. "Yes!" she cried. "Yes, I will marry you!"

They spent the next hour basking in a quiet joy. Sometimes they talked, making plans for their future, and sometimes they sat quietly, enjoying the new closeness they felt. They tentatively decided to get married in two years. By that time, Katie would have only one year left in her nursing program and Steve would be half way through his engineering studies. They agreed that it would be best, in order to save money, for Katie to continue living at home with her parents until the day of the wedding. Diana had been talking about the two of them getting an apartment next summer, but Katie had never made any commitments to her cousin. One big concern they had was whether Katie could transfer all her credits to Steve's college after two years. They decided that on one of Katie's first visits down to see Steve, they would check on that.

"We don't have to decide everything today," Steve said.

"I'm glad. I just want to enjoy this day." Katie held her hand at an angle so the sun's rays seemed to set her ring on fire. "I wish today could go on forever."

Steve put his arms out behind him and leaned back, reflecting. "You know, for most of this past year I've been feeling like I never have enough time for things. I have wished several times that I could live a day, and then live it over again just with you. Like today." He looked lovingly over at Katie. "It's been an awesome day, but you know, if it did go on forever, we would never actually get married." Steve grinned at Katie. "And we would never eat supper! I'm hungry. Come on," he rose while talking, "why don't you get the food out, and I'll start the fire."

Katie jogged down to their 'fridge' while Steve got a fire going with pine needles and twigs.

"What's this?" Katie asked in a surprised voice as she unwrapped a package of T-bone steaks.

Steve glanced up as he added wood to the fire. "You didn't really think I was going to feed you hotdogs and beans for our engagement supper, did you?" He lowered the grate for grilling over the fire pit.

"There are potatoes in the pack in some tin foil. We'll throw them in the fire."

Katie sat back and stared at him in amazement. "You really did a lot of planning and preparing for this day, didn't you?"

Steve reached for the pack and, fishing out the potatoes, tossed them into a corner of the fire pit. "Yes." He continued to dig around in the backpack. He pulled out a citronella candle in a jar, lit it, and set in on the sand next to their towels. "It wasn't all that easy either," he continued wryly. "I practically had to show Gina your ring before I could convince her how important it was for you to have the day off."

"I can't believe this," Katie said, feeling very cherished. "No wonder she smiled at me so mysteriously when I asked for the day off. And when I asked you about Wayne coming – I suppose that was just a ruse when you said he couldn't get off work."

Steve held his hands up in front of him. "Now I never said he couldn't get off work. I told you he couldn't come." Steve's blue eyes twinkled. "He couldn't come because I wouldn't let him."

Katie was still sitting back, trying to take it all in. Her emotions felt like they were on overload. "You are amazing, Steven Reed Anderson, and I love you."

"No, you are the amazing one. My life hasn't been the same since last August when I saw you at the Dairy Shack." He reached for her left hand and ran his finger over her ring. "From now on, whenever anyone comes to Whisper Lake, they'll hear it whispered in the breeze." Steve cupped his hands around his mouth and whispered loudly up into the treetops. "Katie – Katie – marry me – marry me."

Part II

Chapter 15

HOLDING ON

Late October rain streamed down the large windows of the community college's cafeteria. Katie put her lunch tray with its taco salad and glass of cola on an empty round table. Setting her backpack on the floor, she slid onto a chair and, after asking a blessing for her food, began to eat.

"Katie!"

Katie looked up from her lunch to see Wayne approaching her table. He was balancing a full lunch tray on top of a stack of books. Setting his load down, he pulled out a chair next to Katie. His lunch tray was laden with more food than Katie felt she could eat in an entire day. Wayne also said a brief prayer and then dug into his hamburger with enjoyment.

"I didn't know you ever ate lunch here," he said.

"I don't usually, but today I need to spend some time in the library. With the rain and all I just didn't feel like going home in between. What about you?" Katie motioned to all his food. "It looks like you know your way around all the food lines pretty well."

"I eat here every Tuesday and Thursday. I have classes both right before and after lunch."

"How are classes going for you?"

Wayne reached for the saltshaker and sprinkled some on his French fries. "Pretty cool. My Spanish class is a bit of a struggle for me, but I'm doing okay. How about you?"

"I'm doing well. Lots of homework though."

Wayne nodded in agreement and busied himself with eating for a few minutes. Having finished his main course, he slid the plate of chocolate cake into the center of his tray and dove in with obvious delight. "How's Diane?" he asked. "I haven't seen her for weeks."

"She loves her job at the bank and, guess what? She has a boyfriend."

"Some rich dude she discovered at the bank?"

"No. Actually, she met him at church."

"I can't think of a better place to meet someone. So, what's his story?"

"He graduated from high school two years ago. He's a mechanic. Just moved to town in August to work at his uncle's shop. His name is Matt. He's a real nice guy and treats Diana like a queen."

Wayne shoved his lunch tray aside. "Maybe I could meet him sometime. Make sure he's good enough for her." Just then, Wayne's cell phone rang. "Don't go away," he said to Katie. Into the phone he said, "Hey."

Wanting to give Wayne a little privacy, Katie carried their trays to the side of the cafeteria where the return carts were. She dumped the garbage and slid the trays onto the racks. When she returned to the table, Wayne handed the phone to her. "It's Steve. He wants to talk to you, too." Before he released the phone to her, he added, "He's not coming home this weekend."

Feelings of disappointment washed over Katie, but she greeted Steve brightly.

"Hi. I didn't expect to catch you until tonight," Steve's voice carried a warm feeling of tenderness with it. "Lucky for me, you're eating lunch with my bro. I miss you."

"I miss you, too."

"Katie, you know I had hoped to come home after my game on Saturday for the rest of the weekend, but I'm just not going to be able to make it. I have a term paper due next week and I'm way behind schedule. Wayne offered to drive you both down here after work, but I really need to bury myself in the books. I just can't spare the time."

"I understand." Katie closed her eyes. *Would it always be this way?* "Really, I do understand."

Releasing a sigh of relief, Steve said, "Katie, you are the best. Listen," he lowered his voice before continuing, "I sense this is not so easy for Wayne. He expected that he and I would have more time together than we've had this fall. You're emotionally stronger than he is, Katie. Talk to him for me, will you?"

Conscious of Wayne's eyes and ears on her, Katie turned slightly away from the table. "Okay, I'll try."

"Thanks. I have to go. I have class in fifteen minutes."

"Take care," Katie said.

"You too. I'll call you Sunday night. We can talk longer then. By the way," he added, "thank Rachel for the cookies she sent. They were a big hit with the guys on my floor. Tell her we'd like more."

Katie grinned. "Okay, she'll do it, too. She loves any excuse to bake."

"Great, 'bye." Steve paused for just a second before adding with heartfelt meaning, "I love you, Katie."

"I love you, too. Goodbye," Katie pushed the 'end' button on the phone and handed it back to Wayne.

"How do you like that?" Wayne asked, laying the phone on the table. "Doesn't that bother you?" A frown pulled his normally cheerful expression down.

"It's not his fault, Wayne," Katie said softly, defending Steve. "We all knew he would be extra busy this fall. Once soccer season is over his schedule will be much lighter."

"Don't kid yourself, Katie. He'll still be doing intramurals and he'll find some indoor city league to play on."

Katie studied Wayne's face. She had never known that Steve's busyness bothered him. Wayne had always seemed so supportive. He always went along with Steve's agenda. Seemingly, no questions asked. Seemingly, also, to enjoy it. "Once college soccer is done for the season, the rest will be much more low key." Katie tried to encourage Wayne. "He won't have so many practices or road trips."

"Yeah, okay. I know you're right." Wayne's eyes rested on Katie's diamond ring. "That probably makes it easier for you," he said, pointing toward her hand. "Knowing each season brings you closer to having a future with him."

"I didn't say it was easy."

They sat in silence for a minute, and then Wayne picked up his phone and books. "I've got to go."

"I was just thinking," Katie spoke up. "Do you want to hike up to Whisper Lake with me after church on Sunday?"

"What for? It'll be too cold to swim."

Katie shrugged. "I don't know. Just to get away. I don't want us to pack a meal and all that, I just think it'll be pretty up there with all the fall colors."

Wayne stood up, thinking about how much the name Whisper Lake associated itself with Steve. For both he and Katie, going to the lake would be like being with Steve. Almost. *Maybe that's why it's important to her.* "Can I bring my fishing pole?"

"Whatever you want. I think I'll bring a novel and just relax for a while. Forget about school and labs for a few hours."

"I'll bring David and Adam along." Wayne grinned. "We wouldn't want to give people the wrong impression about us."

"That is a very good idea." Katie got to her feet as well and picked up her backpack. "I can spend the day with all of my brothers-to-be."

At the sound of Adam's laughter, Katie looked up from the book in her lap, to the spot where Wayne and the younger boys had waded out to fish. *Such great kids.* Katie smiled at their antics as Wayne tickled Adam in the stomach. David was trying to get them to be quiet, before all the fish were scared away. Katie was not sure there were any fish around today. At least, she hadn't noticed the boys catching any.

She laid her book aside and, pulling up her knees, hugged her legs. She looked at the trees, surrounding the lake. They were dressed in full color: reds, oranges, yellows. It was almost more beautiful now than it had been in August. *Whisper Lake.* Katie cocked her ear.

There was a strong breeze today. Could she still hear her name echoing through the tree branches? *Katie – Katie.* She could imagine Steve whispering to her now. She looked down and fingered her engagement ring. She moved her hand around, so the ring glittered in the sunlight. *Marry me – marry me.* She was sure that the rustle in the trees did sound a little like those special words.

She looked over at the boys. The sight and sound of them pushed her memories to the background. She wondered what else was around this lake. The two other times she had been here, she had never ventured much farther than the spot where she now sat. Looking around, she noticed a trail leading off to the side. Getting up, she took a few steps toward it. Calling to Wayne, she asked him if he knew where it went.

"Goes around the lake," he hollered from the water. "It only takes about a half an hour, if you want to follow it. Comes out over there." Wayne pointed down the beach.

"I think I will. See you guys soon." Katie zipped up her blue sweatshirt. "There had better be fish when I return. I think your mom was hoping to fry some up for supper when we get back."

Wayne waved to her, and then turned to help Adam bait his line again. Katie walked along the path as it turned this way and that, but she always stayed within sight of the lake. She got to thinking about the fir trees that filled the woods alongside of the maples, elms and oaks. Fir trees. Evergreen trees. They were strong and sturdy. Like Steve. She continued her musing as she walked. It seemed like everything made her think of Steve. She was nearing the opposite side of the lake when she saw it. It was a large tree that rose taller than those surrounding it. Actually, it was two trees, but they came out of one trunk. Katie stopped in her tracks and stared at the tree. Now this one reminded her of both Steve and Wayne.

The two trees were separate and individual, but they were joined in one trunk. One of the trees was straight and tall, reaching for the sky. The other trunk was bent. It was not as big around or as tall as its mate was. Katie continued her pondering, as she studied the trees. Two in one. It really made her think of Steve and Wayne's relationship.

The two of them, joined as they were in one family, one name. Like two souls in one. Yet, two individual lives branched out. Steve was like the straight trunk. Pursuing his goals. Always climbing higher. Reaching upward. Touching the sky. Wayne was as the other tree. Seeing his dreams, but not sure how to get there. Not wanting to stray too far from Steve.

Reluctantly, Katie turned from the tree and continued down the path that would bring her back to Wayne and his brothers. She knew that she would remember the sight of that tree. Trees. She knew she wanted to show it to Steve the next time they came up here. She decided they should talk about ways to help Wayne. They needed to encourage him to pursue his music and his dream for traveling. Katie sensed, as she never had before, that Wayne's life was on hold. She just wasn't exactly sure what he was waiting for.

Chapter 16

SOUL MATES

"I'm good for another game, how about the three of you?" Matt, Diana's boyfriend, held a bowling ball in his hands.

"I'd love to play another one," Diana answered, cheerfully.

Katie sat on the bench and began to unlace her bowling shoes. "Two games are enough for me."

Matt looked questioningly at Steve.

"You two go ahead," Steve said. "I'll sit out with Katie. In fact, we'll wait for you in the coffee shop." He stored the bowling balls away, returned their shoes, and paid for their games while Katie visited the restroom. When she came out, she joined Steve in the café. He was sitting at a table for four. Two mugs of steaming coffee were on the table in front of him.

Katie slid into the booth across from her fiancée. "This Christmas break has sure gone by fast," she fretted. "I can't believe I start classes again on Monday. You're so lucky to still have a week and a half left before you need to go back."

"We can see each other some before I go."

Katie nodded and stirred some cream into her coffee. "So, what do you think of Matt?"

"My first impression is that he's a good guy." Steve took a drink of his black coffee. "He seems to care about Diana. They seem happy together."

"I like him, too. And I agree, he is good to Diana, but it's strange."

Steve gave Katie a questioning look. "What's strange?"

"Going on a double date like this with Diana and Matt. After all the things we've done with Di and Wayne." Katie shrugged. "This feels odd."

"Wayne and Diana were never really dating. You know that, Katie."

Katie sighed. "I know, but I always wanted them to. They get along so well."

"Just because a guy and a girl are good friends doesn't mean they'll fall in love. You can't force something like that. It either happens or it doesn't."

Katie did not respond at first. After a few sips of coffee she said, "Well, now Diana has Matt and the four musketeers are breaking up. I feel Diana growing away from me."

"What are you saying? You and Diana are soul mates, Katie. The two of you have this invisible cord that connects you way down deep." When Katie did not reply, Steve continued, "You might be right that Diana is on a different path than you. She and Matt are both working. You and Wayne and I are in college. Life is full of changes, Katie. You need to accept it." He reached across the table for Katie's hand. "I honestly believe that no matter where your lives take you, you and Diana will always be there for each other. Soul mates are for life." Steve motioned for the waitress and asked her to bring a pot of coffee to leave on the table.

Katie let Steve refill her cup and then she added more cream. "Deep down, I know you're right." She tilted her head and gave him a loving smile. "I'm finding out that you're right about a lot of things." She drank a little of her coffee as she thought over Steve's words. "Besides," she continued, "Diana and I are family. Wayne once told me families are forever. Diana and I have a lot of forever ahead of us."

Steve smiled and squeezed Katie's hand. "So do we."

Katie took a few more sips of her coffee before changing the subject. "Let's talk about Wayne. Since Diana's out of the picture, we need to find a girlfriend for him. Then he won't be quite so lonely with you away at school. Besides, maybe the four musketeers can become the six musketeers."

Steve eyed Katie over the rim of his mug and grinned. "Why do girls always have to be match making?"

Ignoring him, Katie went on, "Have you met any special girls at college that we could introduce him to?"

"Katie, look at me." Steve's voice changed from teasing to firm and demanded her attention. "First of all, I haven't met that many girls. I'm not exactly interested. Secondly, has it ever occurred to you that not all guys are like Ryan – chasing after every skirt that comes our way? Some of us are content to sit back until a special girl captures our heart."

"So, you honestly think that no girl has ever captured Wayne's heart?"

"Honestly?" Steve leaned back and seriously pondered Katie's question. His suspicions had never been confirmed, yet he felt a pain twisting deep in his gut. "Honestly," he repeated, "I think maybe once a girl did capture his heart, but she was unavailable so Wayne just let it go."

"Maybe he shouldn't have let it go so easily. Maybe he should have fought for her. I mean did he try to tell her how he felt?"

Steve raked a hand through his hair. Katie recognized this gesture as a familiar habit when he was frustrated, worried or upset. "You don't know what you are talking about, Katie. Life is not a fairy tale. You cannot just make up any ending you want. 'Happily ever after' doesn't fit every scenario." A movement at the entrance to the café caught his attention. "Here come Matt and Diana." Steve squeezed Katie's hand in reassurance. "I love you." He mouthed the words to her as the other couple approached the table. Matt and Diana were laughing, which helped to dissipate the heaviness that had fallen over Steve and Katie.

Matt asked the waitress for two more cups of coffee and for dessert selections to be brought to the booth. After making their choices, the four busied themselves with fresh coffee and pieces of pie.

"So, Steve," Matt initiated the conversation, "Diana tells me you're a soccer star."

Diana leaned close to Katie and whispered, "Actually, I think I said fanatic. Soccer fanatic."

"I heard that." Steve grinned at Diana, then turned to Matt who sat next to him. "Who knows, maybe she's right. Maybe I am a fanatic. I'm going to Pacific Christian College on a scholarship. I guess it does take a lot of time and commitment."

"Do you go on road trips?" Matt asked, genuinely interested, "Or fly to other schools for tournaments?"

"Yes, we do. As a matter of fact, and I just told Katie this when I picked her up tonight, I received a letter from my coach today. Next fall our team is going over to Europe for a week to play in an international tournament."

Matt whistled. Diana leaned back against the booth as she digested this news. Looking steadily into Steve's face, she said, "I would not want to be the one to share that tidbit of information with your brother." Turning to Katie, she asked, "Does Wayne know this yet?"

"No," Steve answered for both of them. "He was at work when the mail came. I haven't seen him yet."

Katie bit her bottom lip as she considered the difficulty of this situation. "Do you want me to break it to him?" she offered.

"No." Steve shook his head. "Thank you, Katie, but I need to be the one to tell him."

For Matt's sake, Diana went into an explanation of how Wayne was the one who had the life-long dream to travel. He had never really been anywhere. Now, Steve, who didn't really care, would be going to Europe. Katie let Diana's words roll over her as she lost herself in her own thoughts. She thought about what Steve had just said about life not being a fairy tale. He was riding on his soccer dreams, working toward a career goal and he had her, the girl who had captured his heart. She looked down at her ring. Steve seemed so content with the promises they had made for a future life together. She wondered if her wedding day would ever actually arrive. She could not help but think that maybe she and Wayne were just chasing after dreams while all of Steve's were coming true. She felt Steve tapping her hand, breaking her train of thought.

"Katie," he said, "did we lose you somewhere? It's getting late. We're ready to go."

Katie focused in on the others. Matt was pulling out his wallet and heading up to the cash register. Diana took hold of Katie's arm, and guided her out of the booth. Pulling her away from Steve, she spoke softly into Katie's ear. "This reminds me of the very first time you and I and Steve and Wayne went to the Pizza Ranch together. Remember? Only this time someone is falling in love with me." Diana's voice radiated happiness.

Katie hugged Diana. "I know. It's wonderful and I'm so happy for you."

Chapter 17

VALENTINE'S DAY

Katie entered her house through the back door and walked into the kitchen. She laid her schoolbooks on the counter and turned on the stove under the teakettle. Humming, she filled the kettle, set it on the burner and then pulled a tea bag out of the canister. Her mom came into the kitchen carrying a laundry basket filled with folded clothes.

"I didn't hear you come in, Katie," her mom greeted her. "Did you see the surprise on the TV set? It came while you were at class."

Katie set the tea bag on the counter and hurried to the living room. Sitting on top of the television console was a bouquet of long-stemmed roses. There were six red and six white ones nestled among baby's breath and ferns. "Oh, Mom, aren't they beautiful?"

Mrs. Fremont had followed Katie to the room. Smiling, she leaned against the doorway and watched as Katie bent over to smell the flowers. "There's a card in there," she informed her daughter before heading upstairs to deliver the clean clothes to the bedrooms.

Carefully, Katie extracted the small envelope from the center of the bouquet and pulled out the card. *To Milady,* it read, *Happy Valentine's Day. Forever, Steve.* Katie picked up the vase and carried it with her back to the kitchen. She set it on the table, got down a mug from the cupboard and finished her tea preparations. Taking her hot drink and the phone with her, she sat down at the kitchen table. Positioning the bouquet directly in front of her, she dialed the phone number to Steve's dormitory room. After the fourth ring, it was picked up and Steve's voice answered.

"I was wondering if there were any knights available to talk to me?" Katie quipped.

"Huh?" Steve asked. He had hurried in from the hall when he heard the phone ringing, and had not yet realized it was Katie. "Night? Who is this? What did you say?"

"It's Milady. I mean, your lady."

Steve sighed, closed his eyes, and leaned against the wide windowsill in his room. All the love he felt for Katie filled his entire being. "Katie."

"I got the flowers. They are so beautiful," Katie said, turning the vase around as she spoke. "Thank you."

"I miss you," Steve's voice was filled with longing as he drew out the words. He opened his eyes and studied a picture of her that was framed and setting on his desk. The picture had been taken during their senior year of high school, the night of the Christmas banquet. Katie was standing in her long lavender dress in front of the Fremont's Christmas tree. Her eyes were alight with promise and hope. "This is crazy, Katie. It's Valentine's Day. I want to be with you."

"I miss you, too."

There was silence on the phone line for a few moments. They weren't speaking words, but their hearts were communicating.

"What do you have going the rest of today?" Steve broke the silence. He glanced at his watch. "It's not quite 3:00. Do you have to go to work?"

"No, I have the day off. I don't work until Saturday."

"Katie," Steve said, reaching a decision. "I'm going to drive home and take you out to dinner. I can be there by six. I don't have class tomorrow morning until ten. I can get up early and drive back down here in the morning."

"Are you sure you can do that? You don't have practice or too much homework?"

"Katie, this long distance stuff is wearing on me. I miss you. I love you. I want to see you."

"I know. It's hard on me, too. I love you, Steve."

"Could you call and make reservations for us at The Iris? I'll take a shower and then I'll be on my way."

"Steve, The Iris is kind of expensive. You already sent the flowers."

"Katie, let me take Milady out for a special night, okay? We don't get to do this very often."

"Okay. I'll call the restaurant, but Steve, I think they require a tie."

"You don't think I own a tie? Knights have a flair for looking good, you know. You put on your fanciest dress and together we'll turn heads."

Katie smiled. Her heart swelled with love. "Consider it done, kind Sir."

A storm had moved in that afternoon. Dark clouds had been gathering since noon and now, at dusk, it was pouring. The rain and the wind pounded against Wayne's bedroom window. Wayne sat on the chair in his room, strumming his guitar. He knew he should be working on his Spanish assignment, but it always seemed to help him concentrate if he spent some time with his music first.

He beat out some fun Beach Boy tunes, then he slowed his pace and began to play many of the songs he and the praise team had done for high school chapels. He missed playing with that group. He missed having a programmed outlet for his music. The melodies filled his soul, as he began to hum and then sing as he played. Closing his eyes, he quietly picked out the notes as he slowly sang again about Jesus being his comfort and strength.

Suddenly his bedroom door was thrown open. Startled, Wayne stopped playing. He opened his eyes to find his mother standing there, looking stricken. "Mom? What's wrong?"

"It's your brother. There's been an accident. The hospital just called."

Wayne set his guitar down. "Who? David? Adam?" He reached out a hand to steady his mother. "What happened, Mom?"

"They said Steve, but how could that be? A nurse from Saint

Luke's here in town called. It must be a mistake. Steve isn't here. He's at school, isn't he?"

"Yeah, Mom. It must be a mistake." He got up and guided his mother over to his bed so she could sit down. "Tell me exactly what they said."

"It was an accident northbound on I-5. It's the storm. There was a pile-up. They said a semi hit his truck. But it can't be." Mrs. Anderson turned pleading eyes to Wayne. "He didn't tell you he was coming home, did he?"

Wayne fell back onto his chair, shaking his head. His thoughts swirled around in his mind. *Northbound. Coming home.* Wayne did not like the way things were taking shape in his mind as he realized it was Valentine's Day. *Katie. Oh, God. No!* "Mom, he must have had a date with Katie. It's Valentine's Day. He must have been coming home to be with her tonight."

"Katie," Mrs. Anderson's voice was just a whisper. "Your father. We need to tell them, and we need to get to the hospital."

"I'll take care of it, Mom. I'll call Dad at the office, then I'll tell Katie." Wayne stood up to leave, then looked back at his mom. "How bad is he? Did they tell you?"

Mrs. Anderson began to sob. "They wouldn't really say. I think they said he's in Intensive Care."

At that point, they heard the garage door, below them, closing as Mr. Anderson entered the house. "Dad's home from work, Mom. He can take you to the hospital. What about Adam and David? Should I tell them, too?"

"No, I'll have your father talk to David and Adam. On your way down, send your father up here, please."

Before Wayne could leave the room, his mom laid a restraining hand on his arm. "I'm sorry to put this on you. It's not an easy thing you're going to do, telling Katie. Please, drive carefully."

Katie took one last look in the full-length mirror in her bedroom. She was wearing a sky-blue velvet dress, with a silver, gauzy-silk jacket over the top. She had done her hair in a loose French braid that hung down her back. Glancing at the alarm clock next to her bed, she moved to the window and looked down onto the street. The wind was blowing in such strong gusts that the rain was coming down almost sideways. It was after 6:30. Steve should have been here by now. Katie reasoned with herself that the weather would have slowed traffic down. He did not carry a cell phone, so he couldn't call her. *Calm down, he'll be here soon.*

Katie went downstairs thinking she should call the restaurant and move their reservations back a little. When she arrived in the kitchen, the sight of her rose bouquet still sitting on the kitchen table caught her eye. She bent over it and drank in the sweet, heady scent of the roses. There was a pounding on the front door. *Finally!* Katie hurried to answer it, relief filling her.

Opening the door, she was surprised to see Wayne standing there. He appeared out of breath, and oddly, considering the raging rainstorm, he was not wearing a coat.

"Hi Wayne," Katie greeted. "I thought you were Steve. He's late. Did he send you over to—?" Katie stopped and studied Wayne's demeanor. "Wayne, what's wrong?"

Wayne had been standing at the door, taking in the sight of Katie, all dressed up, waiting in nervous anticipation for the arrival of his brother. He brushed past her as he entered the room, looking around the front hall as he did. "Are your parents home, Katie? Is your Dad here?"

"No, Wayne, it's Valentine's Day. Dad took Mom out for a night on the town. Rachel's at a thing at church." Katie reached out for Wayne's arm and spun him around to face her. "Wayne," she repeated urgently, "what's wrong? You're scaring me. Where is Steve? Did he get home yet?"

Wayne drew in a shaky breath and looked deeply into Katie's eyes. "I don't know how to tell you this, Katie. There's been an accident. Steve was on his way home, to see you, I guess," Wayne's voice broke. "Oh, God," he breathed an unspoken prayer. "He's bad hurt, Katie. He's at Saint Luke's."

"What? No! But—." Katie groped her way over to a chair in the front corner of the living room. "But, Wayne," Katie crinkled her forehead and shook her head, "he was coming home to take me out to dinner."

Wayne knelt in front of her and took her small hands in his large ones. A tear ran down Wayne's cheek and dripped off his chin. "I know, Katie. I can't believe it either, but it's true. The hospital called a little bit ago. He's in Intensive Care."

Tears gathered in Katie's eyes as reality began to set in. "Is he – is he…?"

Wayne wrapped an arm around Katie's neck and drew her close. "I don't know. I don't know any details, but Katie, we are not going to lose him," he said with determination.

Katie pushed back from Wayne's embrace. "Take me to him, Wayne." She rose from the chair as Wayne also stood up. "Take me to him right now."

They hurried out the front door and down the walk to Wayne's car. He had left the engine running, and, in his panic, had left his car door wide open. The rain had soaked the driver's seat, but Wayne did not even notice as he climbed in. Katie stared out her window, tears streaming down her face as Wayne drove through the dark night and the rainstorm.

Images of his brother flitted through his mind as he drove. There was that time in grade school when Steve had accepted Wayne's dare to put a dozen worms in Sally Cooper's lunch box. He remembered Steve at age thirteen as he rode his bike down the cliff near their house. He had wiped out so badly, he had ended up in a cast with a broken arm. Wayne pictured Steve playing soccer, wearing those colorful goalie shirts with such pride, and then accepting awards in high school for most improved player, most valuable player, and all-conference. Wayne's mind moved to that night at the Dairy Shack and the look on Steve's face the first time he had seen Katie. He pulled himself back to the present, half of his concentration on driving in the miserable weather, the other half on what lay before them at the hospital and how Katie would hold up to this distressing situation. Wayne glanced sideways at her. She was sitting with her head against the door window, silent tears running down her cheeks.

He reached over, took her hand in his and clung to it. "I'm here for you, Katie," he said aloud. He wanted to pray, but in his desperation, he did not know what to pray or even how to pray. He pulled into the parking lot of the hospital and, thankfully, found an empty spot not too far from the entrance.

Wayne waited for Katie to come around from her side of the car, then he grabbed her hand and, together, they sprinted through the rain for the doors of the hospital. Water splashed up around their legs from the puddles pooling in the parking lot. Upon entering the building, Wayne asked directions from the volunteer behind the front desk. Again, he took Katie's hand and led her, at a trot, down the hallway and into the elevator. As the door closed, Katie leaned against the wall.

"I have a very bad feeling about this," she said, tears glistening on her face.

"Katie," Wayne spoke to her in a firm voice, "you have to trust God. Steve's going to be all right."

When the elevator stopped at the second floor, Katie let Wayne lead her down the hall. A sign directed them to the waiting room, where they found Mr. and Mrs. Anderson, David and Adam huddled on chairs in the corner. Wayne's dad rose to meet them and embraced them both in a tight hug.

He explained that Steve was in surgery, but the doctors were not very hopeful of the outcome. He had sustained massive internal injuries. He was unconscious and had been since the crash. Mr. Anderson told Katie that he had taken the liberty of phoning the church secretary to obtain her dad's cell phone number and assured Katie that her parents were on their way.

Nodding her head numbly, Katie wandered over to the large windows across the room. Her clothing, shoes, and hair were wet, but she didn't notice. She stood still, staring out at the dark night. The rain was beginning to lessen.

Wayne's t-shirt was soaked to his skin. He shivered, but walked over to his younger brothers. He sat on the empty chair between them and put an arm around each of them. "It'll be okay, guys," he said quietly, "it has to be okay."

An hour passed. Katie left the waiting room and wandered the halls of the hospital until she came to the chapel. She slipped into the dimly lit room and took a seat. Her mind was in a daze. She could not seem to focus her thoughts. She couldn't even pray.

After she had sat in the quiet room for some time, Wayne appeared in the doorway. Slowly, he lowered himself into a chair next to Katie. He handed her one of the two cups of coffee he held in his hands. "I made some calls," he informed her. "John, Coach, your Aunt Marie. She said she would track Diane down for you."

Katie turned to Wayne, tears brimming in her eyes. For the first time since he had appeared at her door that evening she felt something other than sheer terror. "Thank you," she whispered. "That was very sweet of you." She looked at the coffee in her hand. "You even put in cream." The tears spilled out of Katie's eyes, Wayne's thoughtfulness touching her heart.

"Whatever," he said, staring vacantly into his own cup.

"Katie, Son," Pastor Fremont stood in the doorway of the small chapel. A tear rolled down his face. He walked into the chapel and knelt in front of them. "Steve's gone home to be with Jesus." He put one arm around his daughter, the other on the back of Wayne's neck. "The Lord is my Shepherd…" Softly, Katie's dad quoted the twenty-third Psalm. Tears streamed down Katie's cheeks as she melted into her father's shoulder, but Wayne sat dry-eyed and rigid. He had just lost the most important person in his life. With his usual optimism and hope, he had believed until that very moment that Steve was going to live, but now, he felt empty inside. Nothing mattered to him. Nothing would ever be the same again. Nothing.

Chapter 18

SOMETHING LIKE THIS

Katie stood at the counter in the Anderson's kitchen. It was the day before the funeral. So many friends and co-workers of the Andersons had brought food to the house that it was accumulating on the table and counters. Katie was in the process of choosing something to heat up for their supper and finding freezer and fridge space for other items. She was also putting together a tray to serve coffee and cookies to the many visitors that kept dropping in to offer condolences. Some people only stayed a few minutes; others sat in the living room for hours.

Right now, there were at least four or five people in the living room. Katie wished her mother were here to help her, but Mrs. Fremont had taken all of the Anderson's laundry to her own home to do their washing for them. Katie knew it was a service that would be appreciated. Steve's parents were meeting with their minister and Katie's dad to make the final preparations and plans for the funeral. Katie did not know where David and Adam were. Frankly, she was too tired to care.

Wayne, his brown hair even more tousled than usual, sat morosely at the kitchen table. He had not offered to help Katie with the food. He wasn't even talking to her. As Katie thought about it, she realized that he wasn't really talking to anybody. As visitors came to the house and offered their sympathies to him, he would merely nod in their direction.

Katie heard the doorbell ring. She looked at Wayne to see if he would rise to answer it, even though she was sure he would not. Katie felt she did not have the energy to either. She was certain someone in the living room would answer the door. If they didn't, maybe the people would just go away. She knew that everyone meant well, but Katie was exhausted. She had not been able to sleep well since the accident. She looked up, as the newcomers appeared in the kitchen entryway. It was Diana and Matt.

Diana came over to Katie and silently wrapped her in a hug. She had come every day to be with Katie. Every day, she hugged her cousin as if by her contact she could instill strength into Katie's being. The girls held each other for a long time. Neither spoke. Tears ran silently down both of their cheeks.

Matt leaned against the fridge. He had come to support Diana, but he felt like an outsider here at the Anderson's home. What Diana shared with Wayne and Katie went deep. She shared a history with them, which Matt did not. In fact, he barely knew Wayne.

After a few minutes, Diana loosened her hold on Katie. Stepping back, she took in the scene in the kitchen. Noticing that Katie still held a knife in her hand, she gently took it from her. "Let me do that for you," Diana suggested, pulling the pan of brownies toward her. She finished the cutting job, which Katie had started. "Are you serving these with coffee?" Diana asked in her take-charge manner. At Katie's nod, Diana turned to her boyfriend. "Matt, please look around and find some coffee cups. Put them on this tray, and serve the folks in the front room, okay?"

As Matt followed Diana's instructions, two elderly women peeked around the corner of the kitchen. One held out a package of freshly baked banana bread to Diana. Katie was leaning against the sink, thankful for Diana's assistance.

"Here, dear," the woman said to Diana. "I wrapped it so it could go right into the freezer."

"Thank you," Diana said, graciously.

As the women turned to go into the living room, the second one said in a loud whisper to the first, "Is that the poor fiancée?"

Diana shot a look at Katie, who closed her eyes to hold back the tears. She was so tired of crying. She was so tired of being strong. She was just so tired. Diana opened the freezer and wedged the bread into a small space. "Wayne," she said, looking over her shoulder, "does your mom have a deep freeze somewhere? Not all this food is going to fit in here."

"Basement." Wayne mumbled, his head and shoulders drooping. Diana, raising her eyebrows, exchanged a look with Katie. Katie shook her head. "Well," Diana said, forcing a cheerful tone to her words, "do you want to carry some of this and show me the way?"

"Whatever," Wayne dragged himself off the chair and mindlessly let Diana stack two casseroles and a zip locked package of cookies in his arms. She gathered up some items also and followed Wayne down the steps to the basement. They made a second trip and when they returned, the kitchen was in much better order.

Almost robot-like, Wayne resumed his seat at the kitchen table. Matt, following Katie's directions, was in the process of making another pot of coffee. Diana came to stand beside Katie and leaned against the sink next to her. "Tell me, Katie, is there anything I can do for you? Anything at all?"

Katie turned weary eyes to her cousin. "Yes, there is. Do you think you could contact my professors and explain what's happening? I need a few more days before I return to class. Maybe all of next week. I just don't know right now. I'm so tired I can hardly think."

"Absolutely," Diana said. She reached for a pad of paper and a pen from next to the telephone. "Let's write down all your classes and everything and I will head over there this afternoon. Since tomorrow is Saturday, I better take care of it today." She looked over at Wayne, wondering if he was even paying attention to the conversation. "How about you, Wayne? Do you want me to contact your profs too?"

"I'm not going back," he said listlessly.

"What do you mean by that?" Diana asked for clarification. "Not going back next week, this quarter, this semester? What?"

"I'm not going back," Wayne repeated. "Ever."

Matt, who had finished making the coffee, sat down across the table from Wayne. "I'm not sure you should make such a big decision about your future this soon, Wayne."

Wayne glared at him. "Like you would know."

Katie gasped, shocked at Wayne's insolence. "Wayne," she said, "Matt is just trying to help you."

Wayne turned his brooding eyes to Katie. "No one can help me, Sister." He rose from the table and, bypassing the living room and its gathering of guests, headed upstairs to his room.

Diana stared at Katie. Katie turned around and, leaning over the sink, covered her face with her hands and began to sob. Diana exchanged a helpless look with Matt. He nodded encouragement to her. She placed an arm around Katie, and stood silently by her cousin's side.

Finally, Katie's sobs subsided enough for her to find her voice. "I feel like I've lost both of them, Diana. Wayne is like a brick wall. He won't talk to me. He'll barely look at me. He doesn't do anything."

"Give him time, Katie." Matt's voice came from the corner, where he still sat at the table. "He'll come around."

"I hope you're right," Katie responded as she leaned her head against Diana's shoulder. "I'm okay," she whispered to her cousin. "I'll be okay. Will you go to the college for me? Please?"

Diana scribbled down the information Katie gave to her. "Consider it done. Matt and I will head over there right now. I can come over to your house tonight, if you want me to. Just call me, okay?"

Katie nodded. "Thanks, Diana. You, too, Matt. I'm sorry about Wayne."

Matt rose from his chair and waved Katie's apology away. "It's not your problem, Katie. You have enough on your plate without being responsible for Wayne's behavior. I'll see you tomorrow at the funeral. If there's anything I can do, let me know."

Katie nodded. Diana gave her cousin one last hug. "I love you," she whispered into Katie's ear. "Trust me, it's all going to be okay."

Katie smiled weakly as she watched Matt and Diana exit the room. Wearily, she left the kitchen. She peeked into the living room as she passed. Steve's friend, John, who was attending college in

California, was sitting in Mr. Anderson's leather chair. He had come home this morning and was going to be a pallbearer tomorrow. Katie felt as if she should go talk to him, but she was just too tired. Steve's high school coach, another pallbearer, was sitting on the couch near John.

Katie turned away and headed slowly up the stairs. She went into the bathroom, closed the door behind her and studied her face in the mirror. Her hair was a mess, her eyes were swollen and bloodshot, her complexion was pale. Finding a washcloth in the cupboard, she rinsed it in cold water and held it to her face for a long time. How does one ever prepare for something like this? She didn't know what she was doing. She did not know what she was going to do. Rinsing the washcloth under running water, she looked at her engagement ring. How could so many dreams come crashing down in an instant? *Oh, God, we're in such a mess here. We really need you.*

Hanging the cloth over the towel bar, Katie opened the bathroom door. Her eyes were drawn to Wayne's and Steve's bedroom doors. They were next to each other in the hallway. Wayne's was tightly closed. Steve's was open just a crack. Katie walked slowly toward it and stopped before Steve's door. She nudged it with her foot. It opened, at a snail's pace, revealing a neat, unlived-in room. Most of Steve's usable belongings were in his dormitory room. Steve's roommate, who was driving up in the morning for the funeral, had told Mr. Anderson that he would bring Steve's belongings home.

Warily, Katie entered the bedroom. She made her way over to the desk and sat down in the chair. Not knowing what she was looking for, she opened the top drawer. She noted pens, paper clips, computer disks, and similar paraphernalia. In the corner of the drawer, was a manila envelope. Katie drew it out and emptied its contents onto the desktop. Photographs fluttered across the desk. Katie picked up a few and studied them. Mostly they were snapshots of Steve's family. Goofy ones of the boys. A few from high school graduation. For a long time, Katie studied one of her and Steve, Diana and Wayne. It had been taken the night of the costume/bowling party. They were dressed as Ethyl, Fred, Lucy, and Ricky. They stood with arms around each other, laughing and carefree. Katie felt pain piercing her heart. She thought she could not possibly have any tears left to cry, but they came. In her heart, in her very soul, she cried out to God. She felt as if she was screaming at him.

God had brought her here, from Minnesota. She had thought it was to meet Steve, her life-long partner. What sense was there in any of this? She would have been so much better off if she had stayed in the Midwest. She thought of that old saying; 'It is better to have loved and lost, than never to have loved at all.' She groaned. Whoever said that, did not really have a clue.

Katie laid the picture on top of the others and wandered aimlessly around the room. Touching things; touching Steve's life. She opened the closet door and searched its contents with her eyes. On the top shelf next to a couple of trophies, sat an old, tattered, blue teddy bear. Hanging on hangers were a few dress shirts, a neglected jacket and two old goalie shirts from high school. Katie pulled a brightly colored gold one from its hanger. She held it to her nose and breathed in deeply the smell of outdoors and Steve. She hugged it to herself, and then pulled it on over her head. She ran her hands over her arms. Somehow, wearing his shirt made Katie feel as if Steve was holding her in his arms. She laid down on his bed, pulled his pillow out from under the comforter and wrapped her arms around it. Weeping silently, Katie finally fell into a deep sleep.

Chapter 19

ENDINGS

Katie went into the storeroom of the card shop and approached the office where her boss sat working. Gina was bent over catalogs at her desk, putting together an order. An empty mocha cup sat in front of her and she chewed on a pencil, concentrating deeply. Gina was in her early thirties, with honey-colored, shoulder-length hair and eyes to match. She was a loving and gentle person who had a way of getting to the heart of issues. Katie had enjoyed working for her, and despite the age difference, considered Gina a friend.

"Gina," Katie said, standing in the doorway, "Carol is at the cash register and Shelly is unpacking that new box of cards. Is it okay if I take off now?"

Gina glanced up at the clock above her desk. It read 5:15. "Wow," she said, tossing her pencil down. Stretching, she arched her back. "I had no idea it was so late. Go ahead and clock out."

Katie put her time sheet through the automated clock and stuck it back in its slot. She gathered up her jacket and purse from the corner cupboard. Before she could step away from the counter, Gina turned in her chair and addressed Katie.

"So, it's been, what, six, seven weeks, now? How are you doing, Katie?"

Katie leaned against the cupboard. She bit her bottom lip as she debated what to say. When people asked her this question, sometimes she gave a quick, 'I'm doing okay,' and sometimes she shared how she really felt: tired, hurt, angry, confused, lonely; the list could go on and on.

Noting Katie's hesitation, Gina said, "Maybe I shouldn't have asked. I never know if I should bring the subject up. I never know if the moment is right. I mean, if it's not on your mind at the moment, then I would hate to be the one to put it there and bring the sadness back. On the other hand, I don't want you to think I'm calloused and don't care about you."

Katie set her coat and purse down on the floor. "It's okay, Gina. It's hard to explain, but the truth is, I'm always thinking about it. I mean, even when I'm not; I am. I can be watching a movie, or helping a customer, or doing my homework, but it's always there just under the surface. So, you don't have to worry about making me think about it."

"That must be hard," Gina said, sympathetically. "I suppose as time goes on, the intensity of your feelings will lessen."

"I have mixed emotions about that, too," Katie confided. "At times, I hope that *is* true. I don't think I can go on much longer with the weight of this sorrow. Then again, I don't want to forget Steve. I want to be able to remember all the sweetness without feeling this terrible ache inside of me." Tears gathered in Katie's eyes. "I loved him, Gina. I miss him so much. I just want my life back the way it was."

"Oh, Katie, I'm sorry. I didn't really know Steve. Tell me about him."

Katie closed her eyes and pictured Steve. As she began to talk, she spoke with her eyes closed and a smile on her face. "He had that really short blond hair and the bluest eyes I've ever seen. He had dimples that would appear out of nowhere when he smiled." A tear rolled down Katie's cheek. "He was crazy about soccer. He loved it. No, he *lived* it. He played soccer day in and day out." Katie opened her eyes and looked at Gina. "He was a really good player, too. He went to college on a scholarship."

Gina, sensing that talking about Steve was therapeutic for Katie, nodded for her to continue. Katie pressed her hands together and stared into the corner of the room. "He was really sweet. One time, when we were in high school, I opened my locker in the morning and there was a single yellow rose inside. He always called me his lady, as if he was a knight." A couple more tears freed themselves and escaped down her face. "He loved God. He loved life. He wanted to do everything and I believe he would have." Katie's voice cracked and she paused. "He loved me."

"I remember when he proposed to you," Gina said softly. "He took you up to some lake or something, right? I bet it was romantic."

"He took me to Whisper Lake. He told me that he could hear the wind whispering my name." Katie looked down at the engagement ring on her finger. "I'm still wearing his ring, Gina. Do you think it's time for me to take it off?"

Tears had gathered in Gina's eyes as well. "I think you are the only one that can make that decision, Katie. You'll know when the time is right."

"Thank you, Gina," Katie whispered. "Thank you for letting me talk about Steve. I haven't done that since – well, I just haven't. My sister is too young to understand, and my mom, well, is my mom. My cousin has been the greatest through all this. I could not have gotten through it without her, but she has known Steve for years. Since they were kids. She liked him, but she didn't see him the way I did. Except for those incredible eyes. Everybody was drawn to them. Anyway, I don't think Diana wants to hear the same old things about Steve again and again."

"I bet she would. If she knew it was important to you, I bet she would."

"Yeah, you're right; she's like that." Katie wiped her eyes with the back of her hand. "Steve had a brother he was really close to. Actually, they were best friends. I thought the two of us could talk about Steve together, but –." Katie abruptly stopped talking. Tears pooled in her eyes again.

"But?" Gina prompted.

"See, Wayne was my friend, too, but ever since Steve – since the accident, he's shut himself away from me, away from everybody. It really hurts, Gina, because with Steve there is nothing we can do to make things different. It's final and nothing I can do will ever bring him back. With Wayne, it's different. It seems like such a waste." Katie began to cry again. "He's causing it. He's putting up a wall and he's not letting me in. I lost Steve, my fiancée, and then I lost Wayne, my friend. One makes me sad and the other makes me angry."

Gina pulled a tissue from the box on her desk and handed it to Katie. "He's hurting, Katie, like you are. Maybe he's handling it the only way he knows how."

Katie thought about Gina's words. "Maybe," she agreed. She wiped her eyes and blew her nose. "Thanks, Gina. Talking to you has helped. I think I feel better."

"Anytime, okay? If you remember something about Steve and want to talk about it, please know that I will listen. You can call me at home if you need to. You can even call me in the middle of the night."

Katie smiled and picked up her jacket and purse. "I don't think Dean would appreciate that."

"He'd understand. I mean it, Katie. Anytime, day or night."

"Thank you," Katie smiled appreciatively at Gina. "I'll see you Saturday. Maybe I'll call you before that, but I'll see you Saturday."

Gina patted Katie's back as she passed. "Anytime," she repeated as Katie left the small office.

Katie had to exit the mall near Sears to get to the lot where her car was parked. That meant walking past Rhythm 'n Blues. This morning she had not noticed if Wayne was working. As crazy as it seemed, she wondered if he got copies of her work schedule and made sure he was in the back room of the music store when she would be coming and going. She knew from talking to Mrs. Anderson that Wayne was still working there, but in the past six weeks, she had not once seen him when she passed the store.

She slowed her pace as she neared the storefront. She couldn't help herself from peering in the windows as she passed. Again, there was no sight of him. Katie picked up her pace and then slowed immediately. Sitting there, a mere ten feet away, was Wayne. He was sitting on a bench, staring vacantly at the shoppers walking past.

His hair looked like he had not bothered to comb it that morning and his brown t-shirt was wrinkled.

Katie felt her stomach tighten. She was afraid of rejection, but was determined to get through to him while she had the chance. She eased herself down on the bench next to him. "Hi Wayne," she forced her voice to sound casual. "Are you on a break?"

Wayne turned to look at her as if he had not even realized that someone had sat down next to him. "No, I got off at four."

"Have you been shopping?"

"Nope, just sitting."

"Wayne!" Katie was incredulous. "It's nearly six. Are you telling me that you've been sitting here for two hours?"

"What do you care?"

"I care," Katie said convincingly. "I care about you."

"I wish you wouldn't. It would make things a lot easier."

"Easier for who?" Katie challenged.

Wayne did not answer. Katie sat in silence beside him for a while when an idea struck her. "You blame me, don't you?" she asked in a soft voice. Suddenly it seemed logical to her. "You blame me because he was coming home to see me." When Wayne did not answer, she pursued the issue. "You do, don't you?"

For the first time since they had sat together in the chapel at the hospital, Wayne looked Katie in the eyes. "I don't know, Katie. Maybe I do."

"But that's not fair," Katie pleaded. "You can't hold that against me."

Wayne continued to hold her gaze. "Maybe it's not fair, but right now I don't care."

Katie felt as if he had slapped her. Anger and hurt were rising and she was becoming very conscious of sitting in such a public place. She rose to her feet and planted herself in front of him. "Please walk me to my car." She said it as a directive, not a plea. Turning on her heels, she began to stride down the mall corridor. She did not turn to see if he was following her. Angrily, she pushed open the mall doors and headed to her car at the back of the lot. When she reached it, she turned to look for him. He had followed her, about five paces behind. Katie leaned against her car. Still angry, but not sure what to say to him, she waited for Wayne to speak.

He stood directly before her and put his hands in the pockets of his jeans. "I guess you're mad at me," he stated. "That's probably good. At least it means you feel something."

Katie bit her lip. Instinctively she knew that it would not help Wayne if she lashed out in anger. It wouldn't help her either. Reason. She would try to reason with him.

"I'm picturing something in my mind, Wayne, and I want you to listen and try to picture it, too." She paused and looked at him pointedly. "Are you willing?"

He shrugged his shoulders. "I guess."

The streetlights in the mall parking lot blinked on. The shadows of dusk were deepening as the sun dropped below the horizon. "I'm seeing the two of us sitting on my front porch. It's a Saturday morning almost exactly a year ago. Do you remember?"

Wayne pursed his lips and nodded.

"You made a promise to me. You promised that you would always be there for me, no matter what. You said you wanted to be my friend. You agreed to be my big brother. You said that you would do anything I wanted, be anything I needed." Katie knew that tears were filling her eyes, but she did not want to cry in front of Wayne. She needed to be strong right now. She felt that she needed to press her point here and now while she had his attention. Then if Wayne walked away from her, it would all be over, but at least she would know she had made her best effort. "Well, I need something from you. I need you to be that friend. I need you to keep your promise. It's too much for me to lose both of you." Katie blinked back the tears that threatened to spill over.

Wayne shifted his weight and stared out over the darkening sky. "I can't do it, Katie. You're asking too much of me."

"But why? Why do you have to push me away? We should be comforting each other. This is happening to both of us. We're both hurting."

Wayne looked at Katie and she saw tears in his eyes as well. "When I made those promises to you, I had no idea what it would mean. I didn't know that Steve would be gone." Wayne brushed the back of his hand over his eyes, and again, looked out toward the darkened horizon. "There is so much pain inside me, Katie, so much guilt and confusion. I know you will not understand this, but you are the last person I can share what I'm feeling with. I'm sorry that I can't explain it any better to you."

"Please, just let me be your friend," Katie begged. "I'm on your side in all of this."

Wayne looked at her for a long moment. A single tear rolled down his cheek. "No, Katie, it's not going to work. I'm going to walk away now and I don't want you chasing after me."

Unbidden, the tears rolled down Katie's cheeks. She crossed her arms over her stomach and looked up at the sky, over Wayne's head. "So you're saying goodbye. Is that it? Everything we've had is just over. Because you say so." Katie lowered her eyes to his face. "I'm not going to give up on you, Wayne Anderson. You can walk away from me today. You can toss our friendship to the wind, but you can't force me to do the same. I'm going to be praying for you, Wayne. And I'm going to hope that someday you'll climb out of this pit and you'll discover that you weren't in it all alone."

Wayne pulled his car keys out of his pocket, but would not meet her eyes again. "You're in for a long wait then." He turned to leave, then tossed back over his shoulder, "And don't send Diane over to talk to me. Just let me be."

Katie watched him walk away. He headed down the parking lot. There were not that many cars left in the lot. She saw his black car parked under a light pole about three rows over. When he climbed inside, she unlocked her door and wearily climbed into her own car. She leaned her forehead against the steering wheel and wept. There were so many emotions inside her that she could not sort them all out. When the tears were spent, she leaned back against the headrest and looked over to where Wayne's car had been parked. It was gone. She could not believe he had actually walked away.

Katie turned the key and started her engine. Fiddling with the heater, she turned it on high. She remembered a phone conversation she had had with Steve that fall. It was one of the times when he had not been able to come home for a weekend. He had told Katie that she was emotionally stronger than Wayne was. Steve had always had great insights into people. She started to remember other things he had said to her over the time they had known each other. *What had he said about fairytales? Life is not a fairytale. You can't just make up any ending you want; happily ever after doesn't fit every scenario.* It was almost as if he had known. Katie shivered even though the heater was blasting out warm air. She wished she *could* write her own endings, because this would certainly not be it.

Chapter 20

MEMORIES

Katie, her diamond ring sparkling on her hand, stirred chocolate chips into the cookie dough. She plopped a few into her mouth just before the phone rang. Swallowing the chocolate quickly, she reached for the receiver and answered the phone.

"Katie? This is Lydia Brooks."

"Hello, Mrs. Brooks," Katie greeted. Mrs. Brooks, a woman in her late fifties from church, was very active and loved to be involved with the teens and pre-teens in the congregation. She was the counselor for Rachel's seventh grade Charity Group.

"I'm glad to find you at home, dear. I was afraid you'd be at school."

"I'm finished for the day."

"I admire you, Katie," Mrs. Brooks said. "You are an inspiration to me."

"Why is that?"

"The way you have kept up with your studies after losing your sweet fiancée. I'm sure it isn't easy, dear, but you've stuck with it."

"You're right, it isn't easy, Mrs. Brooks. I just take one day at a time. Finals are in three weeks so the end of this school year is in sight. I suppose what keeps me going are lifelines. Some normalcy to cling to, like school."

"Well, like I said, it's inspirational, dear. Now, to the reason I called. I have an enormous favor to ask you. I've called several women, including your own mother, but everyone has had to turn me down."

Katie's heart sank. This did not sound good. "What is it?"

"You know that I teach Rachel's Charity Group. Such a nice bunch of girls. Friday is their end-of-the-season club outing. The problem is, my sister is scheduled for surgery in Seattle that same day and my husband and I would really like to be there. I'm afraid I won't make it home in time for the girls' outing that evening. I was hoping you could drive them in the church van and chaperone at the restaurant."

Katie smiled into the phone, relieved that it was an easy favor. "It sounds like fun. I'd love to do it. My mom and dad are going to be out of town for a weekend seminar so I'm holding down the fort here, too. It's just going to be Rachel and me all weekend. This will be great. What exactly do I have to do?"

"It's very simple, really, dear. The girls will be dropped off at church a little before six, and their parents will pick them up there again a little after nine. You just need to transport them back and forth to the restaurant and chaperone while you're there."

"Do I have to run any activities?"

"Oh, no. The restaurant has been doing this for years. They give us a great discount on burgers and ice cream. They even take care of the games. We just need to have an adult present at the establishment. It's really very simple, dear. You might even get bored, it's so easy."

"Well, it certainly sounds like something I can handle, Mrs. Brooks. Just plan on it."

"I'm so delighted. I will put your name on the paperwork then. You can pick up the money, van keys, permission slips and all the information from Sally when you come to the church. I would suggest that you are there by quarter to six."

"Okay," Katie smiled. "By the way, how many girls are we talking about?"

"Only nine. The van seats twelve, so there is plenty of room. I just cannot thank you enough, dear. You're very kind."

"It's nothing, really. I hope everything will be all right with your sister."

"Thank you, dear, now we'll be able to stay overnight with my brother-in-law. I'm going to call them right now. Goodbye, Katie."

Friday afternoon found Katie maneuvering through the carpool lines at Rachel's school. It had been sprinkling all day. Maybe she would take Rachel for a treat on the way home. Rachel could have hot chocolate and she could have a mocha. Car length by car length, Katie worked her way to the front of the line. She caught sight of Rachel, standing with a couple of friends. Katie tooted her horn, thinking Rachel was probably used to watching for her mom's van, and might not realize Katie was here in her little silver car. Rachel came hurrying through the rain and, after tossing her backpack into the back, climbed into the passenger seat.

"I forgot it would be you," she said. "I was watching for Mom's van."

"I figured." Katie looked at her sister and smiled before she pulled into the exit lane. "So, how was your day?"

"Not too bad. I got a B+ on my history test. Hannah and I are thinking about trying out for next year's cheerleading squad. What do you think?"

"I think that sounds like fun. You would be good at it. You are very perky." Katie shot her sister a grin. "And you have a loud voice," she teased. Katie pulled onto the boulevard in front of the school. "Do you want to stop on the way home for hot cocoa?"

"You bet! This is going to be a fun weekend, huh, Katie?"

"Of course, just us girls. We don't even have to cook supper tonight since it's your club outing." Katie got to thinking about how enjoyable it would be to spend some time with Rachel's friends at the restaurant. "Say, Rachel," she said, chuckling. "I just realized Mrs. Brooks never told me which restaurant we're going to tonight. Do you know?"

"Of course, the Dairy Shack."

Katie slammed on the brakes. "What did you say?"

"Katie!" Rachel screamed. "You can't just stop here in the middle of the street!"

The man in the car behind her laid on his horn. He rolled down his window and hollered at Katie. "Come on, lady!"

Dazed, Katie put her car in motion again. "Rachel," her voice sounded desperate, "where did you say we were going?"

"To the Dairy Shack. They have ping-pong and pool and foosball tables. It's going to be so fun."

"I can't go there," Katie choked out, her hands trembling. She turned onto a residential side street and pulled up against the curb. She put the car in neutral and turned to Rachel. "I can't go there," she repeated.

"But you have to. It's tradition, Katie. The seventh grader's May outing is always to the Dairy Shack. We've been talking about it all year."

Katie shook her head. "Well, I'm sorry, but I can't do it."

"Katie," Rachel whined, "you promised Mrs. Brooks. What are you talking about, you can't go?"

Katie looked at her sister and bit her bottom lip. "That's where Steve and I met," she confided. "It's where we saw each other for the very first time. I had gone there right after we moved here with Diana and some of her friends. He had gone there with Wayne and a couple of other guys."

"I never heard this story," Rachel said. "Tell me some more."

"Diana and I and some other girls were sitting at a table when these four guys came in. As soon as I saw Steve, I was attracted to him. Wayne told me once that he believes Steve fell in love with me that very night."

"Love at first sight," Rachel whispered dreamily.

"I haven't been back there since Steve died, Rachel. I don't know how I can face going tonight."

"Well, I don't know either, but you're going to have to. Pleeease, Katie," Rachel drew out her plea. "Everyone is counting on you."

Katie closed her eyes and offered up prayer. "Okay, Rachel, okay. I'll think of something. Let's go home. I'm sorry, but I'm not in the mood for treats anymore."

A half an hour later, Katie was on the phone to Diana's bank. She was put on hold, while Diana finished her transaction with a client.

"What's up?" Diana came on the line. "You never call me at work."

"I'm desperate, Di. Please tell me you're not doing anything extra special with Matt tonight."

Diana laughed. "Okay, I'm not doing anything extra special with Matt tonight."

"I'm serious here, Diana. I really need you to come with me tonight." She explained the problem to her cousin, ending with, "I just can't face this alone."

"Wow," Diana whispered. "I'll tell you what; Matt and I were just going over to his brother-in-law's house for pizza and to watch the Mariners' baseball game on Frank's new big-screen TV. I know Matt will understand that I need to go with you."

"Really? Are you sure?" Katie asked, an immense relief filling her.

"Positive," Diana assured Katie. "This is important to you and it's important for me to share with you, to help you. Besides, to be honest, I would love to spend the evening talking with you. Except for at church, we haven't seen each other for a couple of weeks."

"Thank you, Diana. You're the greatest."

Katie sat in the driver's seat of the van in the church parking lot. Nine seventh-grade girls sat giggling and chatting in the back seats. Tapping her fingers on the steering wheel, Katie looked at the clock for the third time in as many minutes. "Come on, Di," she said under her breath. It was 6:10 and the girls were anxious to get underway.

Finally, Diana's car rounded the corner of the church and came to a screeching halt. She ran from her car to the van and breathlessly jumped onto the seat next to Katie.

"Sorry!" She apologized. "My books would not balance."

Katie gave her cousin a wry look. "I was getting really nervous, Diana. These girls were about to lynch me. They all arrived early and have been badgering me for twenty minutes to leave. All of them except Rachel. She's been understanding."

Diana turned to the younger girls behind her. "Thanks for waiting, girls," she called out sweetly, winking at Rachel. "We can go now."

Katie pulled onto the road and began the short drive to the Dairy Shack. "I have a rock sitting in my stomach," she confided quietly to Diana, under cover of all the giggling in the van. "I've been avoiding certain places around town for the past three months. I'm afraid the memories will do me in."

Diana sat thoughtfully for a moment. "Maybe it's time you face your memories," she reflected. "Maybe you need to sort through the pain and the laughter and let go of what hurts and store away what remains. Then your memories can be like a scrapbook or a photo album. You can take them out when you want and they'll bring warm, sweet feelings."

"Those are nice sentiments, Di. I'm just not sure if they'll work."

"Trust me, Katie."

Katie snuck a look at her cousin, and then returned her eyes to the road. "You want to know something, Di? Over the past year and a half, I have grown to trust you. I think you might be right about needing to face my memories head on." Katie turned into the parking lot of the Dairy Shack. There was an open space in front of the main window and she pulled the van into it. Katie breathed deeply. "Anyway, it looks like we're going to find out." She took the key from the ignition and put it into her purse.

Diana turned to the eager girls in the rear of the van. "Okay, girls," she announced. "Go ahead and go in. Katie and I will be right behind you."

While the nine girls climbed eagerly from the side door of the van, Diana studied Katie's profile. Katie was sitting as if in a trance, staring at the front door of the Dairy Shack. "Come on, Katie," Diana put her hand on Katie's knee. "You can do. I'll be right beside you."

Katie forced herself to pick up her purse and the manila envelope that Mrs. Brooks had left for her. "Here goes," she whispered as she and Diana exited the van. Diana went around to Katie's side and took hold of her arm.

"Don't look around when you first go in," Diana advised. "Just march straight up to the counter and get your business taken care of with the manager. I'll get the girls settled, then I'll come back for you."

They followed Diana's plan. Katie pasted a smile on her face as she approached the manager with all the paper work. He was an extremely pleasant man to deal with. He had been expecting the group and took care of the details expediently. Meanwhile, Diana hustled the group of chattering girls over to the large tables reserved for them next to the ping-pong tables. Rachel hung back at first and approached her older cousin. "Diana, will Katie be okay?"

Diana looked her cousin in the eye. "Rachel, you are a very sweet sister to be concerned about Katie, but this is a fun night for you. Katie and I both want you to enjoy yourself. I will take care of Katie. That's what I'm here for."

"Are you sure?"

"Yes, now go on. Well, maybe you could do one little thing. If you happen to notice your sister crying, keep your friends away from our table. Keep them playing games, okay?"

"I can do that, Diana." Rachel seemed glad to have a task for the night, a way in which to help her older sister.

"Good, now join your friends." Diana turned Rachel around and gave her a gentle push.

Katie came over by the table waving a bag that had a drawstring around it. "Here are all your chips for the games, girls. Looks like you can play all you want. They'll bring out the hamburgers after a while."

The seventh graders took over the foosball and air hockey tables. Diana steered Katie toward a small table across from the larger ones that the other girls would sit at. There were roughly fifteen other people in the restaurant. Diana was relieved she did not know any of them. She got glasses of cola for her and Katie, then returned to Katie at the table and slid into the chair opposite her cousin.

"You doing okay?" Diana put the straw in Katie's glass and slid it across the table to her.

Katie pointed to a round table in the middle of the room. "That's where we were sitting that night."

"That's right," Diana agreed. "I was facing the pool table; you were facing the front door and the counter."

Katie turned to look at the entrance of the restaurant, the memories as vivid as if the meeting had been last week. "I remember watching them come through the door. Wayne came in first, then Mike and John together. Steve entered last."

Diana nodded, letting Katie work through the recollections. "I remember being struck by how good looking he was." Katie focused on Diana. "Wayne is good looking too, but there was something about Steve..."

"Wayne talked to me later about how he could almost feel this electrical current running between the two of you – between you and Steve."

Katie looked around the interior of the building. Her eyes rested for a moment on the pool table that Steve and his friends had used that August night. "Diana, I think you were right. It's not as painful as I thought it would be. The memories here are sweet ones."

"Maybe we should continue to free a few more of them," Diana suggested. "After we bring the girls back to church tonight, we could go on over to the Pizza Ranch and sort through the memories you have of that place."

Katie nodded. "That is not a bad idea. Then there's the bowling alley, the soccer field, the high school," Katie's voice trailed off.

"One at a time, girl; we'll conquer them one at a time," Diana said. She could not help herself from looking down at Katie's engagement ring. She wondered how much longer Katie was going to keep wearing it. Diana was not sure she was brave enough to bring the subject up.

Katie took some sips of her pop. "Lately I've been remembering different things Steve said to me. I think when I was going with him, I didn't realize how insightful he was."

"Like what would he say, Katie?"

"It's like he had a better understanding than I did about life. One time he told me that life is full of changes and I needed to accept that. I think about that now. At the time, we were discussing something totally different than this situation, but it's almost like he knew."

Diana nodded and let Katie continue with her reminisces. "He talked about being open to God's will." Katie's eyes became moist from unshed tears. "He taught me a lot of things, Diana. I think that during the year and a half I had with him, I went from being a girl to becoming a woman. When he first died, I wished I had never moved here, had never met him, because then I wouldn't have had to suffer so much pain. But now," a single tear trickled down Katie's cheek, "now I think of how much he brought to my life and how much he taught me." Katie quieted and turned to thoughts inside her heart that she did not want to share with Diana.

Diana let Katie sit and reflect. She noticed the waiter bringing out trays of burgers and fries so she went to help settle the girls down at their tables and sort out their meals. When she handed Rachel a cheeseburger she leaned over and whispered in her ear, "I think your sister's heart is doing some healing tonight, Rachel. I think coming here was part of God's design."

Rachel and Diana looked across at Katie. She sat pensively at her table. Perhaps she was praying, they could not tell. Rachel smiled at Diana. "Thank you," she said, with heartfelt appreciation for more than just the food.

Diana brought the remaining burgers and fries over to the table she shared with Katie. She placed some in front of Katie and salted her French fries. "Are you hungry?" she asked Katie.

Ignoring the food and Diana's question, Katie looked down and fingered her ring. "I think it's time I let him go," she said in a soft voice.

Diana stopped pouring ketchup onto her fries. She eased the bottle back down onto the table. "What's that?" she asked with care.

Katie bit her bottom lip, took a deep breath and said with determination, "It's time. Gina told me I would know. I don't think there will ever be a better time or place." Katie nervously turned her ring around on her finger before she resolutely twisted it off. Reverently, she laid it on the table in front of Diana.

It was a rare moment in Diana's life for she did not have a clue what to say. She stared at the ring in front of her. She had known

Katie needed to do this. She had also known that it had to be Katie's own decision. Now, the deed was done, but neither of them knew where to go from here. Diana looked up at Katie's face and offered a tentative smile. "You've done the right thing, Katie," she whispered.

"Take it for me, will you?" Katie closed her eyes. "Keep it safe for me, Diana. Someday I'll ask for it back, but I can't carry it home tonight."

Slowly, Diana picked up the diamond solitaire. She got out her wallet and placed the ring safely in the zippered coin section. For both girls, it felt like the ending of a very long chapter in a book. Now that the ring was off her hand and Katie had learned that her memories were not all filled with sorrow, she seemed relieved. Her mood brightened a little bit and she unwrapped her burger.

"Thank you, my friend. I could not have done that without you."

"I am glad to be here to help you, but you did it on your own, Katie. I believe with all my heart that you're going to be okay."

Chapter 21

PRAY FOR ME

It was nearly ten o'clock on Saturday night. The light inside the house was dim since Katie had left only a few lamps burning. Classical piano music drifted softly from the stereo in her bedroom. The door to her room was standing wide open. It had just been a little over twenty-four hours since Katie had taken off her engagement ring and given it to Diana. Now she was in her pajamas, on top of the covers on her bed. She lay on her back, looking across the foot of her bed where a picture of Steve hung on her wall. It was the framed article and photo of him from the school newspaper taken after his team had been to the state tournament. He was dressed in a goalie shirt and an excited grin was on his face.

"I miss you, Steve," Katie stated aloud to the picture. "I went to the Dairy Shack with Diana last night."

Suddenly Katie sat up. She was sure she had heard creaking on the stairway. She swung her feet over the side of her bed and her heart began to race as she heard a footstep on the landing.

"Katie!" Diana's voice called as she came down the hall to Katie's room.

"I'm here," Katie quietly called back, relief filling her. She waited for her cousin to enter the bedroom. "Be quiet, Di. Rachel's sleeping."

"Katie Fremont," Diana scolded, as if Katie was a child, "you should have the doors locked, with your parents gone."

"I know, I was going to go do it soon. What are you doing here?"

Diana tossed off her denim jacket and sat down on the end of

Katie's bed. "You have *got* to talk to Wayne," she announced. "Have you seen him lately?"

Katie shook her head, "Not for several weeks. Why?"

"I'll tell you why." Diana was talking agitatedly, so Katie crept over and shut her bedroom door. Diana continued, "Matt and I went to an early movie at the mall tonight. When we came out, we went over to the food court to get a late dinner. We saw Wayne there eating by himself, so we brought our food over to his table and asked if we could join him."

Katie cringed. She had a pretty good idea where Diana was going with this.

"He was so rude to us, Katie," Diana went on heatedly. "He actually said he would rather that we ate someplace else. And that's not all! You should see him. You would be appalled. He looks awful. He needs a haircut and it looked like he just threw on any old clothes. I mean, does he go to work looking like that?" Diana paused for just a moment as she pictured Wayne. "It's such a shame. I always thought he was the handsome one. I think the worst part is his eyes and the expression on his face. You know how he was always so full of fun? And his eyes had that teasing look all the time? Well, now there's nothing, Katie. Just dullness." Diana stopped talking and studied her cousin's face. Katie's green eyes were filling with tears and her face held a knowing look. "You don't look surprised, but you said you haven't seen him for weeks."

"I haven't," Katie answered. "He won't let me see him. The last time I saw him was about five weeks ago. He was having a rough time. He told me then that he couldn't be my friend. More or less, he told me to stay out of his life."

Diana's jaw dropped open in surprise. "I didn't know this! You never told me that you had a conversation like that with him."

Katie looked past Diana to Steve's picture on the wall. "I guess that's something else I learned from Steve," she commented. "Not to break trust."

"What?" Diana asked. "What does that mean?"

"You know," Katie explained, "not to divulge other people's

confidences."

Diana turned around and looked at Steve's picture. "He really was a special guy, wasn't he?"

"Yes, he was. Diana, I'm not really surprised about what you said about Wayne. I've suspected that all the life has gone out of him, but I'm praying for him. I just hope that with enough time, he'll come around."

"I think you should try talking to him again," Diana urged.

"It won't work, Di. I've tried calling the house. He just has his mom tell me that he doesn't want to talk."

"How about if we go over to the Rhythm 'n Blues shop sometime? He can hardly run away if he's at work."

"Diana, think about it. Do you honestly think it would be fair to him to get into that type of a discussion at work?"

"Do you think it's fair to just let him keep throwing his life away?" Diana countered.

Katie sighed. "No, I don't." Katie quieted as she thought about the situation.

"How about church then?" Diana persisted. "You and I could go visit his church some Sunday. He does still go to church, doesn't he?"

"I honestly don't know. I hope so." Katie flopped back on her pillows. "Diana, we are not just going to show up at his church. I know this is hard. I realize that seeing him tonight was unsettling for you, but I have been thinking about Wayne for weeks. I am going to honor his request to stay away from him, but I'm going to keep praying for him."

Diana let Katie's words sink in. "I'll pray too, but I'm going to keep my eyes open for an opportunity to talk to him. You know me, Katie. I always have wanted to stick my face into everybody's business if I think it needs to be fixed."

Katie tossed a small square, decorative pillow at Diana. "That's an understatement! Say, where's Matt? Is he waiting downstairs?"

"No, after that fiasco at the mall, I had him drop me off at my house so I could get my car. I wanted to come right over here and talk to you. I knew I would never get to sleep if I didn't."

"Want to borrow some pj's and sleep over?" Katie asked. "We can go down and fix some tea. Rachel made cookies today."

"That sounds fun, Katie. We haven't slept over together since the winter of our senior year."

Katie found a nightgown for her cousin to wear, then hurried down to the kitchen to put the kettle on to boil. She was pouring English breakfast tea into large blue mugs when Diana came downstairs. Diana raised her eyebrows, "Breakfast tea? Aren't we going to go to sleep at all tonight?"

Katie shrugged. "It's good, especially with French vanilla cream and a little sugar."

"Oh, I see," Diana grinned as she watch Katie finish fixing their hot drinks. "This is like dessert tea."

"I guess," Katie giggled. Diana carried their mugs of tea over to the table while Katie got out some of Rachel's famous double chocolate fudge cookies. Diana pushed some papers aside and sat down by the table. "This is fun. I should abandon Matt more often and come stay with you."

Katie sat down on a chair across from her cousin and nibbled on one of the cookies. "You and Matt have such a different relationship than Steve and I did. You two are almost always together."

"That's true," Diana agreed, "but you have to remember that we are out of school. There's no homework or sports or stuff like that competing for our time."

"Good point. You guys also have money, since you both work. Sometimes Steve and I could barely scrape up enough for pizza. I remember one time in the spring of our senior year we pooled all the coins we could find in our vehicles. We had exactly two dollars and eleven cents. It was just enough for two cups of coffee and a donut each at the Glazed Shop."

Diana sipped her tea and studied her cousin's face. "It's good to hear you talk like that. I think you're climbing out of that gully you were thrown into."

Katie sat quietly and drank her tea. "You don't see me when I'm all alone," her voice was barely above a whisper. "You don't hear me cry myself to sleep at night."

Diana put a hand on one of Katie's. "I meant *beginning* to climb, Katie. I didn't say you've reached the top. I think going to the Dairy Shack last night and taking off your ring were tremendous steps on the climb up. I think you're going to make it."

"It's true what you say about last night. I am glad to discover that my memories can be sweet, but it's very hard." Katie reached across to the papers by Diana's elbow. She picked up a pamphlet from the top of the pile and laid it in front of her cousin's cup. "I'm going away to school next fall, Di," she announced calmly. "I'm going back home to Minnesota."

"What do you mean?" Diana felt as if the wind had gone out of her sails. "You're leaving?"

"Yes, there is a very good Christian college in Minneapolis. They have an excellent nursing program. I've checked on everything. All my credits from this year will transfer."

"I'll miss you, Katie. I have loved having you here so much."

"You don't need me, Diana," Katie said resolutely. "You have Matt now, and a good job. With Steve gone and Wayne, well," Katie faltered, "it's too hard for me here. I want to get a fresh start. Minnesota still feels like home to me."

Diana bit her bottom lip. "I don't like it, Katie, and I will hate saying goodbye, but I think I understand." The girls sat in silence for a few minutes, then Diana spoke again, "I guess for the past nine or ten months God has been mapping out a different road for each of us to follow." Tears pooled in Diana's brown eyes. "I am sorry, Katie, that yours has been so difficult."

"Pray for me, will you, Diana?"

Diana nodded, a tear trickling down her cheek. "You and Wayne both," she promised.

Chapter 22

A BROTHER

It was late afternoon on one of the first days of June. There was not a cloud in the sky and the temperature had reached 80 that afternoon. Katie was driving home from class with the car windows open and a light heart. She had finished her last exam that day; she felt happy for the first time in a long time. There were still things that she needed to work out, but for today, at this moment, she felt good. She pushed up the three-quarter length sleeves of her light-blue shirt. She wished she had known the morning mist was going to break; she would have dressed for warmer weather.

Katie turned north onto Maple Avenue. Every so often, as if her car had a will of its own, she found herself driving home past the Anderson's cul-de-sac. Today, she turned into the entrance of the city park that was just two blocks from their house. The clear blue sky and the warm sunshine beckoned to her. She parked near the tennis courts and took a walk down around the playground and the empty wading pool, ending up next to the baseball diamond.

A few kids were out on the field, playing fliers up. Katie sat on the bottom row of the bleachers and, closing her eyes, lifted her face to the sun. She sat quietly for a few minutes, letting the sun warm her.

"Katie!" Katie's heart lurched and she opened her eyes to see Steve's youngest brother, Adam, running toward her. A baseball lay about six feet in front of her. Adam picked it up, turned to throw it back to his friends, and cautiously approached Katie.

"Hi, Slugger," Katie greeted him slowly. "I didn't know you were out there."

Adam, dressed in blue jean cut-offs and a blue and white striped t-shirt, stopped directly in front of Katie. He scrutinized her face. "You don't look any different," he announced.

"I don't?" Katie asked in all seriousness. "Should I?"

"When I asked Wayne why you never come over to see us anymore he told me 'cause everything is different – even you."

Katie felt her stomach begin to churn. "I think what he meant, honey, is that I feel different inside."

"Don't you like us anymore?"

"Oh, Adam," Katie put her hands on his shoulders. "I love you. David too."

"Wayne too?"

Tears filled Katie's eyes. With one hand, she fingered Adam's blond hair. It was sweaty from play, but so much like Steve's had been. "Wayne too," she assured Adam in a soft voice. "Very much."

"Then why haven't you come over? I know you mostly came because you were going to get married to Steve, but I miss you, Katie."

The churning in Katie's stomach worsened as a familiar anger made its presence felt. Wayne had put up this wall and now his youngest brother was suffering for it. Katie had tried to call Wayne a few times, but he always sent the message back to the phone that he didn't want company. She had not seen him for weeks. Except for running into Wayne's mom at the gas station once, she had not seen any of the Andersons for quite awhile. Mrs. Anderson had expressed her concerns to Katie that Wayne was becoming increasingly withdrawn. Katie had never realized how far-reaching his grief or this situation between her and Wayne would be.

"Adam, sit here beside me, okay?" Katie patted the bench next to her. "I'm going to explain something to you that is kind of grown up. Do you think you can try to understand?" At Adam's solemn nod, Katie continued. "You know that I was going to marry Steve. I was so happy about becoming your sister. When Steve died, it changed a lot of things, but not my love for you. It's been really hard for everybody with him gone, hasn't it?" Adam nodded. "We all miss him very much, don't we?" Another nod. "Well, I think that it is especially hard for Wayne. And you know what makes it even harder for him?" This time Adam slowly shook his head from side to side. He was hanging onto Katie's every word. He slipped his small hand into Katie's and she gave it a squeeze. "I think it's extra hard on Wayne when he sees me because I remind him so much of Steve. It's easier for Wayne if I stay away. Does that make sense to you?"

"Yes, Katie. By staying away you're trying to help make it easier for Wayne."

Katie put an arm around Adam. "That's right, Adam. I'm sorry. I didn't know that it was making it harder for you. We could see each other sometimes though. I can't come to your house, but we could meet here at the park. Would you like that?"

Adam's eyes lit up. "Do you know how to throw a baseball?"

"I'm not sure. Can you teach me?"

"Okay, that'd be great, 'cause Wayne won't play with me. He used to be a lot of fun, but not anymore."

"What does he do, Adam?"

"He goes to work sometimes. He goes to church on Sunday. I think that's all. He's in his room most of the time."

Katie closed her eyes. *Oh Wayne.* She felt her heart breaking. The anger dissolved. Pity took its place. Hearing a commotion on the field, Katie looked up to see Adam's friends waving and hollering. "I think it's time for you to go," she told him. "It's almost time for supper. Adam, you can call me to meet you here sometime if your mom says its okay. Maybe Sunday afternoons are good."

"Okay!" Adam jumped down. "'Bye." He began to run off to meet his friends, but then turned when he was several paces away and yelled back to her, "I'm going to tell Wayne that you're not really any different." With that, he continued on his way. He hooked up with the other boys and together they headed home.

Sighing, Katie got to her feet and went back to her car. She started the engine, but did not put the car in gear. *Father God,* she prayed, *did you bring me here today to help Adam? That sweet little boy who could have been my brother? I wanted a brother. I've always wanted a brother.* A tear formed and rolled very slowly down Katie's cheek. *I wanted those brothers.* A still small voice spoke in Katie's mind. *You have a brother.* Ignoring the thought, which did not make sense to her, Katie reflected on how hard it was for those three boys to lose their brother, especially Wayne. The voice in her mind spoke again. *He has a brother, too.* Katie shook her head as if by doing so, she could chase away the thoughts that had come unbidden. *You have a brother.*

Katie pushed in the button that turned on the car's radio. She had it set on a Christian station. The DJ was just finishing a traffic report and announced that it was time for more music. *Good,* Katie thought, wishing to clear her mind. First piano music, then the strong voice of a woman singing filled the car. Katie's mind was riveted to the words of the song. Her eyes filled with tears. She knew this song; they sang it often in church. As she sat silently, the words spoke to her as the singer sang about how Jesus is her brother, even though he is a king.

Katie reached over and turned off the radio. *You have a brother.* Katie began to cry. God certainly was persistent with his message. She remembered too, a verse in Hebrews 2 that says Jesus is not ashamed to call us brothers. He was all the friend and brother she needed. *Thank you, Father, for my brother Jesus.* She prayed for Wayne then. She prayed that God would reveal the brotherhood of Jesus to Wayne, too. *In His time,* she thought, *in His time.* Katie sat and prayed for a while longer. When she finished, she felt better than she had in months. God had not abandoned her. He had even given her a brother to walk beside her.

Chapter 23

SECOND TIME

Katie and Rachel sat on their wooden porch swing. Moths buzzed around the porch light overhead. It was an evening in early August and it was still warm outside, even at nine o'clock. The sisters sat in their shorts and t-shirts. Rachel was barefoot, but Katie had on her sandals.

Rachel held a game on her lap. It was a small board game where one person hid colored pegs and the other person had to guess the pattern. Rachel was thinking aloud as she tried to figure out what fit and what didn't.

"Let's see," she murmured thoughtfully, "green has to go there and red must go someplace." Her voice trailed off as she fiddled with the pegs in her hand.

Katie idly pushed the swing with her foot. She took a sip from her glass of lemonade that was setting on the porch railing. "Take your time, Rachel. You can figure it out." At the sound of a car slowly coming down their road, Katie looked up toward the street. Rachel was still focused on the game.

Katie set her glass down and felt her stomach drop to her feet as the black car crept to a stop in front of their house. "Rachel," she said urgently, "take the game and go into the house."

"Why?" Rachel asked, looking up at Katie. She followed her sister's gaze toward the road. The car's door opened and Wayne emerged.

"Please, Rachel," Katie pleaded.

"Okay," Rachel scooted off the swing and, carrying the game, scampered through the front door, letting the screen door bang behind her. Katie watched Wayne as he cautiously approached the house. She was thankful to see that his hair, though messy, had been recently cut. He wore faded jeans and a plain white t-shirt; a pewter cross hung from his neck on a leather strap. As he neared, Katie could see that he still wore a haggard look. He appeared to have lost more weight and his eyes and face still lacked their usual vivacity. Permanent circles seemed to have taken up residence under his eyes.

When Wayne was about halfway up the walk, he spotted Katie sitting on the swing. Locking his brown eyes on hers, he walked the remaining steps, until he reached the bottom of the stairs. Hesitating a moment, unsure of his welcome, he slowly mounted the steps. At the landing, he leaned against the white pillar that supported the porch roof. He and Katie had not yet broken eye contact.

Nervously, Katie hooked her long hair behind her ears. She was so happy to see Wayne. Her heart was beating furiously, her stomach beginning to churn nervously. The last conversation she had had with him was the one in the mall parking lot back in April, four months ago.

Wayne shoved his hands in the front pockets of his blue jeans. He cleared his throat and, with his eyes burning a hole in Katie's, said, "I came over to say goodbye."

Katie felt the bottom drop out of her world. He had finally come over to see her, but he had just come to say goodbye. Hadn't he already said goodbye to her at the mall that night last spring? "I don't understand," she said softly, studying his face.

Katie noticed tears filling Wayne's eyes and though he no longer held contact with her eyes, he was studying her; his gaze swept across the length of her body, her face, and the long blond hair that cascaded about her shoulders. He seemed to be committing her features to memory.

"I'm going away for awhile." His eyes returned to hers. "I leave tomorrow."

Katie closed her eyes, a lump forming in her throat. "Where are you going?" she asked, opening her eyes and forcing her voice to remain level.

Wayne shifted his weight. "Tomorrow I'm flying to my Uncle Brad's in San Francisco." His voice was flat, defying emotion. "My uncle has arranged to take a few weeks off work. We're taking his camper and going to do some traveling."

Katie stared at him. She could not believe it. This is what Wayne had been wanting to do for years, ever since he was a fifth-grade boy in geography class. It was the starting point of his dreams. Katie patted the place on the swing that Rachel had vacated. Infusing enthusiasm into her voice, she invited Wayne to sit beside her and tell her all the details.

Reluctantly, Wayne moved from his place at the top of the steps. Unhurriedly, he lowered himself onto the bench seat, but intentionally sat away from Katie so his leg would not brush against hers. Katie twisted on the seat so she could face him.

Looking at her, he began to explain, "My parents set this whole thing up. They've been really worried about me." Wayne paused as he gathered his thoughts.

Into the stillness Katie inserted, "Diana and I have been worried about you, too."

"I never meant to cause anyone worry. It's just that it has taken all my strength to go through the motions of living the past six months. I kept my job, but everything else just doesn't seem to matter."

As the sun moved a little closer to the horizon, the shadows across the front yard lengthened. "Your trip?" Katie gently prodded.

"Yeah," Wayne crossed one ankle over his other knee. "My folks have been doing a lot of talking with my uncle. He and I have a pretty good relationship and they decided it would be best if I spend some time with him and do a little traveling for a while. They haven't really given me a say, except..." Wayne stopped talking. He looked across the yard toward the street, then took a deep breath and continued, "Uncle Brad wanted to go ahead with our South America plans, but I refused." He gave Katie a piercing look. "I can't go there after planning that trip with Steve."

Katie nodded in understanding, but remained quiet, hoping Wayne would continue to talk. He rubbed his hands across his thighs. "I convinced them that I'm fine with just exploring the States. We're going to spend a few weeks going across country, just camping and taking it easy."

Katie smiled wistfully. "Don't you see, Wayne, you're about to take off on your dreams? This is the start for you."

"Don't you see, Katie," he said reproachfully, "what it has cost me? We both know that I would not be going now if Steve was still living."

"I know," Katie whispered. A stillness settled over the two. Words seemed pointless. They rocked gently for a few minutes, both of them fighting tears. Katie was the first to break the silence, "I probably won't be here when you get back."

Surprised, Wayne looked at her sharply. "Where would you be?"

"I'll be leaving around the twenty-second of August. I'm going back to Minnesota. I'm transferring schools."

Wayne shut his eyes and held them closed for a long minute. Regret flooded his entire being. "Okay, then," he said slowly, "we'll each be going our own way. Do me a favor, will you?"

"Anything," Katie promised.

"Keep praying for me, okay? I'm struggling with a lot of things, Katie, but I haven't given up on my faith. Maybe your prayers are what's holding me to the cross." He chanced a look into her moist green eyes. "Maybe it's the knowledge that it's all I really have left."

A tear rolled down Katie's cheek. "And will you pray for me?"

Wayne nodded. Feeling that he had to know how things stood with Katie and her relationship to Steve, he reached for her left hand and, holding it briefly, looked at the back of it. Quietly, with a bit of wonder in his voice, he said, "I see you took off his ring."

Unbidden, a few more tears joined the first down Katie's face. Not sure how Wayne felt about her action, she whispered her answer tremulously, "It was time."

Wayne nodded again. Gently, he laid Katie's hand on her lap and released it. "I also wanted to thank you for spending some time with

Adam. He's told me that you've met him at the park a couple of times to play catch. It means a lot to him. It means a lot to me, too." Wayne rose from the swing. When his weight lifted off, it sent the swing in motion.

Katie had to force her arms down so they would not reach up to hold him back. "Why don't you stay and talk awhile?" She dared to ask. "I often think about what you said in April about feeling guilty and confused. I've felt that way myself and besides, I have a pretty good listening ear if you want to talk about anything."

Wayne looked down at Katie on the swing. "I just came over to say goodbye, Katie. I couldn't leave tomorrow without doing that. I'm sorry, but nothing has changed. Everything I told you that night at the mall is still true. I can't talk to you about all the stuff I'm feeling and thinking. I can't mourn with you and I can't be the brother you wanted. I can't even be your friend," his voice cracked as he turned to leave. He climbed to the bottom of the steps, and then he turned back. In a low voice, he confessed, "It should have been me."

He continued down the front walk and climbed into his car without another backward glance. He sat motionless behind the steering wheel of his car in the gathering twilight. Perhaps he should not have said that last line to Katie. Maybe it was too much to lay on her. He believed it though with all his heart. Steve was the one who had everything going for him; besides, he was the flesh and blood son of the Anderson's; and even more important, he was the one with the rightful claim to Katie. Wayne turned his head toward the Fremont's porch. He could see Katie sitting in the light of the porch. He ached to still be sitting beside her on the swing. He could not tell for sure from this distance, but since he saw her wipe her hand across her face, he was pretty sure she was crying. Crying tears that he had caused. He wished that he could be the one to wipe them away.

For her part, Katie's eyes had followed Wayne down the walk and into his car. She watched him as he sat, looking at her from the safety of his car. The words he had spoken last kept echoing in her mind. *It should have been me.* Katie wiped away the tears on her face, but more fell. Briefly, she wondered how many more months she would spend crying. It said in the Bible that God would wipe away every tear. *Father, you must be getting pretty tired of wiping mine away.* The engine to Wayne's car started. Katie's eyes were glued to the car window so she noticed when Wayne, in a gesture of farewell, laid his palm against the window for a moment before he pulled away from the curb. Before he drove out of her life for a second time.

Chapter 24

ANDERSON

Wayne had always felt at home in his Uncle Brad's San Francisco townhouse. The apartment was decorated with souvenirs from many of Brad's trips. Such things as a small statue from India, a nesting doll from Russia, arrowheads from Texas, pewter candlesticks from Scotland and dishes from Japan were on display on shelves and tables. As a boy, Wayne had been impressed with his uncle's collections and had hoped, someday, to begin his own.

Now, Brad and Wayne sat at the kitchen table. Dirty supper dishes had been pushed to the back and an atlas was spread out in front of them. A pot of coffee was on the table and Brad held a steaming cup in his hands. Wayne was mindlessly spooning sugar into his mug, as he followed Brad's finger across the map.

"So," Brad was explaining, "as you see, we can either head south to Bakersfield and then go through Arizona, New Mexico, Texas, and so on until we get to Little Rock or Memphis. At that point, we should probably head north and make our way back. Or," Brad moved his finger on the map, "we could just cut across California right away and go into Nevada and Utah. We could keep heading east until we get to Kansas City or St. Louis." Brad, his dark hair graying at the temples, leaned back in his chair and drank deeply of his strong, specially brewed coffee. "It's up to you, Wayne. What sounds the most interesting?"

Wayne, putting his coffee cup to his lips, looked over the rim at his uncle. "You know what? I really don't care."

Brad sighed and looked down at the map. "Okay, then, I'll choose the route. At least to start. I say, let's head east right away. The southern route will be very hot this time of the year, and there's no air conditioning in the camper. I think you'll like Nevada and Utah, anyway."

"Fine with me."

Brad laid his black reading glasses on the table and elbowed the map a little closer toward Wayne. "Check it out. Is there any place you really want to see?"

"Nope," Wayne was still having trouble getting excited about this trip. "Whatever."

"Okay, we'll get groceries tomorrow and get the camper ready to go. We'll do church on Sunday, then at the crack of dawn on Monday, we're out of here." Brad closed the atlas. "I like to grill a lot when I'm camping and I drink a lot of coffee on the road. Anything special you want?"

"Don't worry about me," Wayne answered. "I'll go along with whatever you plan."

Monday morning found Brad and Wayne traveling the roads from San Francisco to Carson City and across backcountry roads in Nevada. Wayne took only a minimal interest in the things they saw and the places they visited. Early Tuesday afternoon they had stopped to poke around at a place called American Canyon. Now it was barely even a ghost town, but in the 1880's it had been a thriving mining camp filled with thousands of Chinese miners. As Wayne wandered aimlessly among the ruins, he imagined the many men that had scraped out a hard living in that camp. He thought about the men who would have come there as part of a family clan; about brothers who had mined side by side; about the men, who in all likelihood, had died there.

"Let's go," he suddenly called to his uncle as the images pressed in too close.

Brad had been surveying a broken down mine shaft. "Fine," he readily agreed as he headed toward the truck. Brad was willing to let

Wayne dictate their agenda whenever he wanted to. He knew that his nephew was sorting through intense emotional issues and Brad was confident that God was not finished with the boy.

Near sunset a few evenings later, they were camped along the river in Zion National Park in Utah. Brad was at the picnic table reading a newspaper that he had picked up at a store earlier that afternoon. Wayne, lounging in a lawn chair, was studying the way the light danced across the canyon walls, which rose in a circle around the campground. It was amazing to him, how in a matter of minutes, the walls of the canyon changed in color. He reached for his guitar and quietly strummed a couple of worship songs. As always, the music soothed his spirit. Between the music and the beautiful surroundings, Wayne felt something begin to stir deep in his soul.

However, as they motored through county after county, the same thoughts ran through Wayne's mind repeatedly. *It should have been me. Steve was the true Anderson.* He felt a tremendous amount of guilt weighing him down. Steve should be the one alive. He was the one so close to achieving his dreams. Wayne felt he had no right to chase after his dreams anymore. Dreams of traveling, teaching school, coaching.

One hot afternoon, as they traveled across Colorado, Brad shook Wayne's shoulder to wake him up. "I'm pulling off for gas. You want anything?"

Wayne rubbed his eyes. "Yeah, coffee, maybe. Do you want me to drive for a while?"

Brad agreed, so after they had filled the gas tank and climbed back into the cab of the truck, Wayne took his place behind the wheel. He held a Styrofoam cup of bitter coffee in his hand. Brad took a drink of his own and grimaced. "You just can't get good coffee in these out of the way places," he commented. Wayne grunted but kept his eyes on the road. Brad leaned slightly against his door and studied this nephew of his, his sister's only child.

"You know, Wayne," Brad spoke up. "Maybe I should say a few things to you. I know you've been struggling since February and maybe you don't want any advice. You probably want to work it all out on your own, but sometimes it helps to have somebody to talk to. Let me ask you a question. You know all those praise songs you're always playing on your guitar? Do you mean the words that you sing?"

Wayne shot a look at his uncle. "You know that I do."

"Well, Wayne, God is not false. He doesn't change and his faithfulness continues. Think about it. There's something else too. I can see the questions spinning around and around in your mind, day after day. Sometimes there just aren't any answers. Once in a while, you simply have to let go and let God be God." Brad silently drank the rest of his bitter coffee. Tossing the cup in the small, plastic trash bag that hung from the radio dial, he spoke up once more.

"I guess we never have talked about the time when your folks died." Listening, intently, Wayne set his coffee down in the cup holder of the dashboard. He gripped the steering wheel tighter, but did not say anything. "I would have taken you in," Brad reassured his nephew. "I offered to, in fact. Wayne, the Andersons really wanted you. They said you were already like a son to them, like a brother to Steve. I knew they could offer you so much more than I could, as a single man. With them, you not only had a dad, but also a mother and brothers. David was just a baby then and Adam hadn't even been born, but you and Steve were already inseparable. They wanted you, Wayne. They still want you." Brad paused to give the message time to sink in. Wayne took his eyes off the road for a moment to focus briefly on his uncle.

"You aren't just *like* a son to them," Brad continued, "you *are* their son."

Silence filled the cab of the truck. Brad prayed for his nephew while Wayne chewed on his uncle's words. Wayne had turned twenty years old that summer; which meant he had spent more years as an Anderson than a Martin. The memories of his real parents had faded so that he could only recall glimpses of them. Whenever he thought of family, he automatically thought of Dad and Mom Anderson, Adam, David, Steve...He tapped the steering wheel. He would always think of Steve as part of his family. He knew that what Brad had said to him was true. Dad and Mom had never, in twelve years, treated him any differently than Steve or David or Adam. He had always received as much love, care, and discipline as the others. Wayne could not stop a smile from forming at the corners of his lips. Well, perhaps he had received a bit more disciplining than Steve had, since his mischievous ways tended to land him in more trouble than his brother. Of course, more often than not, Wayne had dragged Steve into trouble with him. Like the time they had put the container of earth worms in Mrs. DeYoung's desk drawer in fourth grade.

Wayne took his right hand from the steering wheel and, deep in concentration, rubbed it down his right thigh. How had Steve once worded their relationship? The two of them were a packaged deal...had been... *Oh God, I miss him so much!* Their family would never be the same. Why, for the past six months, had it been so hard to remember pleasant things? Why had he felt such a desperate churning in his stomach? He missed Steve. A lot. His life had lost direction and he hated the fact that he had not be able to say goodbye to his brother, his best friend, his confidante...Why had Steve done it? Why? Why had he gotten in that truck and driven home on that terrible stormy night? In the middle of the week, no less! After all the weekends he had had excuses NOT to come home, why had he come home THAT night? *Oh, man!* Startling Brad, Wayne pounded the dashboard. His desperate thoughts continued, *I am so mad at you, Steve! I am so mad at you...and...and... Katie!* Wayne felt sick to his stomach and his eyes were filling with tears of anger and frustration. Noticing an exit ramp off from the highway that led to a picnic site next to a river, he made a last second decision, and, almost too late to do it safely, swerved the pick-up truck down the exit ramp. Pulling haphazardly into a parking spot, Wayne slammed on the brakes and came to a stop too quickly. Punching the release button to his seat belt at the same time that he forced open his door, he turned teary-eyed to a shocked Brad and sputtered, "I can't drive anymore! I am so mad at them!"

Wayne half fell, half jumped, out of the cab of the truck and staggered, blinded by his tears, toward the river's edge. Turning, he stumbled along the rocky bank as far as he could, perhaps 300 yards, until a cliff blocked his way. Slamming his fists against the rock wall before him, he slumped to his knees at the foot of it. The tears he shed were the first ones he had cried since his brother's death. "How can I be mad at him?" Wayne called aloud to God. "If I were him, and I had been engaged to Katie, I would have done the same thing and driven home to see her that night." Tears subsiding, Wayne turned and sat on the ground, looking out toward the river. That was not a true comparison to make, he realized, because if he had been engaged to Katie, he would not have been attending school 130 miles away. He shook his head. Nevertheless, Steve had done things differently than Wayne would have. In addition, really, how could he be mad at Katie? Because God had moved her to Washington? Because she had fallen in love with Steve, and Steve with her? How could he be mad at Katie for things beyond her control? His stomach churned with emotion. How could he be mad at Katie, when he really just wanted to love her? Wayne threw up his hands in surrender to God, to the Father that he loved and worshiped. He prayed for a long time and let God speak to him and sooth his aching heart.

Thirty minutes passed before Wayne looked back toward the wayside picnic area. He saw his uncle, about 40 feet away from him. Brad, squatting on the bank of the river, held a closed book in his hand, and prayerfully, kept watch over his nephew. At Wayne's glance, Brad stood and approached Wayne. "You okay?"

Wayne motioned for Brad to sit beside him on the rocks. "For months now I have felt as if I've been stuck, like in quicksand. I couldn't pull myself out and I sometimes wondered if God was going to leave me floundering forever."

Brad held up his small travel Bible. "Can I read you something from Isaiah?" At Wayne's nod, Brad put on his glasses and located the verses he wanted. "Chapter 43, this is the Lord speaking, '…I have summoned you by name; you are mine. When you pass through the waters I will be with you; and when you pass through the rivers, they will not sweep over you. When you walk through the fire, you will not be burned; and the flames will not set you ablaze.'" Brad closed his Bible. Wayne felt God's Spirit washing over him as he mulled over those beautiful verses of hope and assurance in his mind.

"All my life, I've loved God," Wayne proclaimed to his uncle. "When my folks died, God got me through it. I can't believe God could ever make a mistake, and I also believe He has everything in His hands. So...all I can really do is trust Him to get me through it this time, too." Wayne picked up a small handful of pebbles and tossed one into the river. "You know, ever since Steve died, I thought my dreams had died too. I guess I didn't feel as if I had any right to live my life, when he couldn't live his anymore." Wayne tossed a few more pebbles into the water. "You know what I just realized? For years, I've been keeping my dreams simmering, but I never went after them. Even when I started college last fall, you know, to start on my education courses, I felt as if I was just filling my time in between Steve's games and doing stuff with him. Doing stuff *for* him. Steve never wanted to travel anyway. I mean, what was I thinking? What have I been waiting for? I've spent my entire life, living Steve's dreams. I thought I was happy doing that. I thought that's what God wanted me to do." Wayne turned to his uncle and looked deeply into Brad's light brown eyes. "You know what, Uncle Brad? I want to live. I want to live *my own* life."

Chapter 25

KATIE AGAIN

Two mornings later, when they were camped near the western border of Kansas, Brad stepped out of the camper to discover Wayne making breakfast on the camp stove. Strong coffee was perking and Wayne was humming as he laid strips of bacon on the griddle.

Wayne looked up and cheerfully greeted his uncle, "Well, good morning, sleepy head." They both knew this was a joke. Every morning since they had left San Francisco, Brad had been the first one to get up and cook breakfast. Wayne had dragged himself out of his bunk at Brad's call and would only eat a little food before downing a few cups of coffee.

Brad grinned. *What a great day,* he thought. For the last two days, he had been observing a transformation in his nephew as Wayne sloughed off his depression and regained some of his zest for life. He could see the light coming back into his dark brown eyes, and the way the boy was eating again, Brad was hoping he would soon see Wayne gain back the weight he had lost.

"Hey, get the map out, will you?" Wayne asked as he turned the bacon. "I want to see where we're headed today. I think I'll call home, too."

Brad glanced at his watch. "You'd better wait until we stop for lunch, it's too early yet."

"Oh, yeah," Wayne said. "Time change. I forgot."

At the truck stop where they had lunch later that day, Brad bought a newspaper. "Go make your call," he told Wayne. "I'll pull a lawn chair out of the camper and read the paper."

While his uncle settled down to catch up on the news, Wayne took his cell phone and wandered across the parking lot, which was full of semi trucks and found a quiet spot where some grass and a few trees grew. He punched in his home phone number and waited impatiently until his mother answered.

"Hey," Wayne greeted her.

When his mother responded, he could tell that she was both surprised, and pleased to hear his voice.

"I wanted to let you and Dad know that I'm doing okay now, Mom." He paused to gather his thoughts. "Uncle Brad has helped me and I've worked through a lot of things. I'm starting to feel like my old self again. I don't have everything sorted out yet, but I'm making progress."

He knew from the sniffles coming through the line that his mom was crying. They talked a while longer, Wayne enthusiastically telling her about the places he was seeing and where they were headed next. He figured that he and Brad had nearly two weeks before they would be coming back into Washington. Assuming his dad was at work, he asked if his younger brothers were home.

"David's at a friend's house," his mom informed him, "but Adam's here. Hold on and I'll get him."

While Wayne waited, he lowered himself to the ground and crossed his legs. "Hi, Pal," he greeted his brother when Adam came on the line. "What's up with you?"

"Well, yesterday Mom took me school shopping. I got a Mickey Mouse lunch pail. He's surfing and a big wave is coming up behind him."

"Sounds cool," Wayne nodded. "What else is new?"

"David and me got gerbils! Mine likes to run around on his wheel. The first night he kept me awake all night, so Mom moved them to the family room."

Wayne chuckled. "Gerbils, huh?"

"Yeah, Katie said they were cute." Adam dropped Katie's name into the conversation as if it were a natural thing.

Wayne's heart skipped a beat. "Katie?" he asked, fishing for more.

"She came over the other day to see Gordon, my Gerbil. She left yesterday." Adam had a way of sharing information with Wayne that sent his heart and head spinning.

"What do you mean, she left yesterday? I'm not understanding you, Adam. Do you mean for school?" Wayne looked at the date displayed on his watch and did some fast calculating in his head. "It's too soon for that."

Wayne could picture Adam shrugging as his little brother answered, "Yes, for school. She said she wouldn't be back home until Christmas. That's a long time, isn't it Wayne?"

"It sure is, Pal. Hey, put Mom back on, okay?"

"Yeah, sure. When are you coming home, Wayne? I want you to see Gordon."

"I'm not sure. Probably in a couple of weeks. Just pet him for me, okay? Now, please, get Mom." Wayne picked up a twig from the ground and broke it into several pieces as he waited for his mother to return to the phone.

"Yes, Wayne? Adam said you wanted to talk to me again."

"He said Katie left for school. I thought she wasn't leaving for a few days yet."

"She and Rachel and her parents left yesterday. They decided to drive out to Minnesota and spend a week with friends of theirs before they drop Katie off at college. You know, it's only been two years since they moved from there. I imagine they have a lot of people they would like to see."

"Oh, sure," Wayne's voice faded away. He did not know why it should matter to him. He had known that she was going and he was not going to have gotten home in time to see her off anyway. He looked across the cobalt blue Kansas sky. It was disturbing to him not to know where she was.

"Wayne?" Wayne realized his mother had repeated his name for the second time. He shook himself to clear his thoughts and lighten his mood before he answered. "Really, Mom," he teased her, "gerbils, huh?"

"The boys needed something."

"Yeah, I s'pose. Tell David and Dad that I say hi." Wayne paused then added, "Love you."

He turned off his phone and made his way back to the truck. Brad looked up, over his reading glasses, as Wayne stopped in front of him. "Well," Brad asked, "what's new at home?"

Wayne stuck his hands in the back pockets of his cargo shorts. "The boys got gerbils. Adam named his Gordon."

Brad grinned and folded the newspaper. "Anything else?"

"Katie left for college yesterday."

Brad looked at his nephew with raised eyebrows, "Katie?"

"Yeah, you know," Wayne said, "Steve's Katie."

That night, after the supper dishes were done, Brad was crinkling newspaper to use as fire starter. Wayne was digging through the cab of the truck. Shutting the door and carrying the atlas, he came around to the picnic table and opened the book to the section where the entire United States was displayed. Laying it on the tabletop, he turned to Brad.

"Hey, Uncle Brad," he said. "Come here. You know how you asked me if there was any place I wanted to go?" He waited until Brad joined him at his side. Brad fished in his shirt pocket for his glasses and put them on. He followed Wayne's finger as Wayne pointed to a spot on the map. "Right there," Wayne informed him. "That's where I want to go."

"Minnesota," his uncle stated. He wondered briefly why out of all the places possible, many of them with more attractions than Minnesota, his nephew picked that state. "Okay," Brad said slowly, "we can do that. It's just straight north of where we are now." He looked at Wayne. "May I ask why or which part?"

Closing the atlas, Wayne explained simply, "It's where Katie's from."

"Ah, I see," Brad restrained a smile. "Katie again. What part of Minnesota would that be, Wayne? It's a pretty big state."

Wayne shrugged. "Doesn't really matter. Southern, I guess. She's from the southern part. I don't where, exactly. I just want to see it."

Brad nodded in understanding. "You like this girl, huh?"

Wayne put a foot up on the bench of the picnic table and took just a moment before answering. "Well, yeah," he confessed. This was the first time that he had ever openly admitted it. "But she's Steve's girl."

Brad slowly took off his black glasses and returned them to his shirt pocket. "Son," he said kindly, placing a hand on Wayne's shoulder, "she's not Steve's girl, anymore."

Wayne looked at his uncle. He stared into his uncle's light brown eyes for a long time, as the information sank in. He did not answer Brad, but gave him a thumbs up and wandered off to sit on a camp chair. He wondered when his feelings for Katie had begun. His *more than friendship* feelings.

Brad, sensing Wayne needed some quiet time to think, went back to his fire making. As the sparks ignited and the flames grew, Wayne wrestled with his feelings. He had to admit it, as he thought back to that very first night two years ago at the Dairy Shack, that if electricity had not been racing between Steve and Katie, he probably would have asked her out. But when had his own feelings deepened? Wayne mulled it over. Maybe it was on all those trips to away soccer games. He had escorted Katie to almost every one of them. They had always had fun, talking and laughing in his car, on the way to and from the games. He did not know when it had happened. He had not meant for his feelings to grow. If Steve had lived, Wayne would have continued to suppress them. However, he had known for a long time that he felt something special for Katie. The feelings were sweet, but they had become a burden.

Chapter 26

HOMEWARD BOUND

From the Colorado-Kansas border, Brad and Wayne headed the camper east across Kansas to Kansas City, and then they traveled north. Their goal was Minneapolis, Minnesota. From there they planned to trek west across the southern section of the state and begin to make their way back to Washington, where Brad would deliver Wayne, before he drove home to San Francisco.

Wayne climbed into the cab of the pickup after a break to stretch their legs at a roadside rest area in Missouri. Laughing, he handed a paper plate filled with cinnamon rolls to Brad.

"Where'd you get these?" Brad asked, his mouth watering at the sight of the rolls, dripping with frosting.

"I can't believe how many friendly people there are in this country." Wayne shut the truck door and strapped on his seatbelt. "I got to talking to this elderly couple. That's their RV." He pointed across the parking lot. The large motor home had Texas license plates on it. "Anyway, when the lady found out we were two poor bachelors traveling alone, I guess she felt sorry for us. She said she had just baked a batch of these this morning."

Brad grinned and nodded his head. "Well, what are we waiting for? Where's that thermos of coffee?"

Brad and Wayne poured themselves cups of coffee and sat enjoying the treats before starting up the truck engine. Swallowing the last bite of his second cinnamon roll, Brad said, "Okay, here's the plan," he outlined for his nephew, "at each rest area you wander around and scout out all the nice little old ladies and go into your poor old bachelor routine. I'll keep the thermos filled with fresh coffee."

Wayne reached for his third, and the last, roll. Tearing it in half he offered part to his uncle. Brad shook his head and patted his stomach. "You're the one who needs it, Wayne. Go ahead and finish it."

"Okay," Wayne grinned, "but how come I have to be the one to approach all the little old ladies? You could take a turn. I do know how to make coffee, you know."

Brad turned the key in the ignition and pulled out of the parking lot. "That's true," he granted, "but I think the sight of a gangly, underfed, twenty-year-old is going to soften a lot more hearts than a gray-haired fifty-year-old."

"Okay, but if we find any widow ladies, then you're on."

A few nights later, they were camped near Mankato, Minnesota. Wayne was intrigued by this state that Katie called home. The Land of Ten Thousand Lakes. It was pretty, he had to admit, but it was very humid and not only were there thousands of lakes, there were thousands of mosquitoes, too. He slapped at another one on his leg and put his guitar on his lap. As he picked out a tune, he wondered where Katie was.

He looked overhead at the stars that were starting to appear in the night sky. She was probably here in Minnesota as well, maybe even looking at the same stars right now. He wished she was here with him. He wished he could talk to her about all the neat things he was seeing. He wished he could go back to having her as a friend, but he did not know if that could ever happen. He could not just put her in a friend compartment in his mind anymore. He knew that he loved her, had indeed loved her for a long time. He had come to understand that that was one of the reasons he had walked away from her before. Twice. Wayne grimaced and rubbed his hands down the tops of his thighs. This was a hard spot to be in. It was indeed very hard to love Katie so much, and not be sure what to do about it. *Father, show me the way...*

Reflecting the intensity of his emotions, Wayne began to strum his guitar in earnest. Brad was sitting at the picnic table, under the light of the lantern, playing solitaire with a worn deck of cards. Wayne played a couple of songs when, out of the corner of his eye, he noticed two young girls, perhaps twelve years old, standing, shyly, at the corner of the campsite. They were listening to his music. Wayne waved to them. "You can come on over," he invited. "Do you have any favorites?"

The girls slowly came into the campsite and sat on the ground next to Wayne. He played while they sang. Before too long, an older couple passed by walking their poodle. They, too, stood nearby and listened. Brad invited them to join the others. An hour passed. At the end of that time, there were close to fifteen people gathered around Brad's campfire, singing along while Wayne played.

Wayne finished the last song and laid his guitar carefully on the grass next to him. "That's it, folks," he said. "Thanks for coming by."

Brad stood up and shook hands with the men. The woman with the poodle told him that she would drop by with some muffins in the morning. Brad and Wayne exchanged good-humored smiles. When the last of their fellow campers left, Brad sat down in a lawn chair next to his nephew and put his hand on Wayne's knee.

"That was great," Wayne said. "We even got muffins out of it."

"I'm proud of you," Brad said seriously. "I told your mom before we left that you would come back to us."

Wayne looked at his uncle in the flickering firelight. "It was a long journey," he admitted. "I regret a lot of it. I wasn't very nice to some of the people that care the most about me."

"Everyone handles grief in their own way, Wayne. Don't beat yourself up over the past. It's what you do from here on out that really counts."

Wayne nodded. "I know, but that's what I'm still trying to figure out."

Several days later, Brad and Wayne were walking back to the camper after picking up some small trinkets for David and Adam in the gift shop at Mount Rushmore.

"I've been thinking," Brad said. "It's the first of September. I think we need to skip Yellowstone and head home down Interstate 90. As much as I'm enjoying this trip with you, I am going to have to get back to work. We're a couple of long days away even if we take the interstate all the way home. Then I still need a day to get back down to San Fran."

"It's okay, Uncle Brad," Wayne assured him. "You've been great. This trip has been more than I ever thought it would be. We've seen so much and met a lot of great people. I can't believe how many different states we traveled through." They reached the truck, and opening the door to the camper, set the bag of souvenirs inside. "I understand, Uncle Brad. We have been gone a long time. I appreciate what you've done for me."

Brad laid a hand on Wayne's back. "I'd do it all over again. In fact, I think some day we will."

Wayne grinned. "Sounds like a plan to me. Say, would you mind driving a while yet? I'm tired. I think I'll try to sleep some, then I can drive late tonight if you want."

"Okay," Brad agreed. They went around and got into the cab of the truck. Wayne rolled up a sweatshirt and stuck it behind his head, against the window.

A few hours later when he woke up, it was late afternoon. He opened his eyes and, still leaning against the sweatshirt, looked out the window as he tried to clear the cobwebs from his mind. The nap had felt good, but now his brain was muddled.

Brad was cruising down the interstate. Wayne stared mindlessly out at their surroundings. Slowly, it began to dawn on him that the sides of the highway were filled with flowers. Hundreds of flowers bloomed along the ditches of the road. Yellow flowers with black centers. Wayne did not normally do well with flower names, but from somewhere in the back of his mind, a name came to him. Black-eyed Susans. Then he remembered. This is what Katie had talked about in one of the first conversations they had ever had. She had told him about the Black-eyed Susans that grow wild across Montana. Sitting up, he tossed the sweatshirt on the floor. He looked ahead of them, and then across to the other side of the freeway.

"Hey, Uncle Brad, are we in Montana?"

"Yes, we crossed the border a couple of hours back."

Wayne relaxed against the seat and thought about Katie. He pictured her in his mind. He remembered the conversation they had had at the Pizza Ranch when, in her poetic way, she had told him about the flowers growing in Montana. He remembered, too, how he had told her that someday when he was crossing Montana and saw the flowers for himself he would think of her. Wayne turned and stared out the window. Back then; when he had flippantly made that remark, he never dreamed that someday he would find himself in a situation like this. Loving her. Needing her.

He thought about what his uncle had said to him several days ago. As hard as it was, Katie was not Steve's anymore. He could hardly dare to hope that she might return his feelings. She had feelings for him, he was sure of that, but they were feelings for friendship, not love. Wayne recalled the night he had gone over to her house to say goodbye. He had picked up her left hand to see if she still wore her engagement ring. She had not been wearing it. As he realized the significance of this, a tiny bit of hope began to stir in Wayne's heart.

"Are we going to stop soon?" he asked Brad.

"Why? Are you hungry?" Brad glanced at the clock in the dashboard. "We can have an early supper, then you can drive a few hours yet."

"I don't care about supper. I need to write a letter."

Brad pondered Wayne's statement. In four weeks, the boy had only sent one postcard to David and Adam, had only called home twice, and now he suddenly needed to write a letter. "You know, Wayne, if we drive late tonight, we'll make it home by tomorrow night. You'll beat the letter back to Washington."

"I'm not sending it there."

"Oh?" Brad cast a quick look in Wayne's direction.

"It's to Katie. She's back in Minnesota."

Brad rubbed his left temple. "Well, we just came through there a few days ago. We could have stopped to see her."

"I wasn't ready then. I think a letter would be best. Anyway, I don't even know where she is. I'll have to call her cousin and get an address."

"Tell you what," Brad proposed, "we still have some steaks in the fridge. At the next rest area, I'll cook supper and you can write your letter, then mail it at the next town when we stop for gas."

"Thanks," Wayne said, mesmerized by the flowers along the roadside.

Forty-five minutes later Brad and Wayne were at a rest area. Brad set the cook stove and grill on a picnic table near where the truck was parked. He rummaged through the camper's fridge and cupboards until he found enough things left from their dwindling supplies to fix for supper.

Wayne took a notepad of yellow legal paper and made his way across the grassed area to a table further down from where the cars were parked, in the shade of a large oak tree. He settled down on the bench, and putting pen to paper began, thoughtfully, to write.

Dear Katie,

Ever since Valentine's Day, I haven't been able to stop thinking about you, especially since I left. I hope and pray that you are okay, and settling into dorm life at college. I'm sorry I didn't write sooner, but as I told you last spring, I wasn't ready. You were probably right when you said we should be comforting each other, but it was something I had to work out by myself.

Actually, I'm sorry for a lot of things. Things I did and didn't do. Things I did and didn't say. I know that you were on the receiving end of most of those things. Now I feel that I am ready to talk about it, to share with someone. Well, not just anyone, but with you. So many things need to be said between us. Things that need to be put right. My heart aches. I'm wondering if yours does too...

Wayne paused in his writing. He chewed on the end of the pen as he thought about how much he wanted to commit to paper and how much he wanted to wait and say to Katie in person. Formulating ideas in his mind, he bent over the paper again and finished the letter.

Chapter 27

ONCE UPON A TIME...

Katie opened her eyes and wiped away the tears that had run down her cheeks. During the past two years of her life, she had gone from one emotional extreme to the other. She had experienced a lot of joy, but also much pain. Reading the beginning of the letter from Wayne had brought it all back. She had not allowed herself to remember everything for several weeks now.

Returning to Minnesota for college had been a good idea. At least here, there were not so many visible, daily reminders of Steve...and Wayne. She had tried to start anew. She had not set out any photographs or mementos from the two years she had lived in Washington. She had not even told Sara, her new friend and roommate, anything important from that era, but now this unexpected letter from Wayne had changed everything. One little letter and all the memories came flooding back. Of course, she had to be honest with herself. Wayne's letter may have been unexpected, but it was certainly hoped for. She had never given up on him. She had prayed daily that he would come out of his depression and find himself. She had also kept a candle flame of hope flickering in her heart that someday he would come back, not just to himself, but also to her. She needed his friendship.

Wayne's letter offered her hope. Katie laid the pictures of Diana, Wayne and Steve on her desk and picked up the letter from her lap. Setting it down on top of the photos, she smoothed it out. With her heart growing lighter, she leaned over her desk and finished reading the letter.

...So many things need to be said between us. Things that need to be put right. My heart aches. I'm wondering if yours does too. It took me a long time, but I finally learned something that I suspect you knew all along: the hardest part of loving someone is letting them go.

I'm moving forward with my life. It has been a long six months, but I'm beginning to see the light at the end of the tunnel. This trip has been so much more than I ever dreamed possible. I can't wait to tell you about it.

I need to see you, Katie. I'm in Montana now, on my way home. I have some things to take care of when I get there, but then I am going to come to see you. I hope to be in Minnesota by the first of October. I don't want to wait any longer than necessary. I will call or email the exact dates as soon as I know them.

Until then,
Pray for me as I pray for you – Wayne

Katie's heart soared with expectation. Wayne was coming to see her. Maybe they could bridge the gap that had formed between them and rebuild their friendship. Katie was not sure how she could wait three weeks.

Her thoughts were interrupted as the door to her dormitory room was slowly opened and Sara poked her head in. "I've got the mochas and bagels. Can I come in? Did you finish reading your letter?"

"Yes!" Katie cried, jumping off her chair and opening the door all the way for her roommate. Sara was balancing a wrapped bagel on top of the lid of a cardboard cup, one in each hand. The bagels were toasted with raspberry cream cheese filling. "Thank you!" Katie took one set from her friend.

Sara placed her cup on the desk and turned to study Katie's face. "You look different," she observed. "There's a light in your eyes that I've never seen before."

Katie, bagel and drink in hand, sat on her bed. She motioned Sara to sit on the other end. "If you have time, I have a story to tell you."

Sara joined Katie on the bed. "Only if you want to, Katie."

"I do want to," Katie said decisively.

"If you're sure, then I have time to listen. I would love to get to know you better." She rose from the bed. "I'll just lock our door so we won't get interrupted."

Katie took a few sips of her steaming mocha as Sara settled back down on the bed. With a faraway look in her eyes, Katie began, "It's a very sweet love story. One that could begin like all good stories with 'Once upon a time there was a knight and his lady,' but I'm afraid it does not end 'and they lived happily ever after.'"

During the telling of Katie's two years in Washington, Sara was a silent listener. She got caught up in the emotions of Katie's life story. She grieved for her new friend. She had had no idea that Katie had arrived at college with so much sorrow behind her. Listening to the last part about Wayne saying goodbye before he left for California broke Sara's heart.

Katie stopped talking and looked out the window. The sky was still overcast, but the rain had stopped. It was getting a little bit dark outside. The cafeteria would soon be open for the supper meal. She turned to her roommate, who had a tear drying on her face. Katie reached over and patted Sara's knee. "Then I came here," she concluded. With a genuine smile, she added, "And then you brought in the mail." She got off the bed and picked up the letter from her desk. She pressed it between her palms. With a light sparkling in her green eyes, she briefly told Sara the main points of Wayne's letter.

"So he's coming to see you. You're excited, I can tell."

"Yes," Katie acknowledged. She walked over to the window and looked down from her second floor perch. She could just make out the doors of the cafeteria. She watched several students as they headed in that direction. "He's coming to visit me, but I guess I can't expect things to be the way they were before. It will all be new territory from here on out. I live here in Minnesota now, and I don't know how to be Wayne's friend without Steve being part of the picture."

"Katie," Sara said fondly from the bed, "is that all you want from

Wayne? All you expect from him, is just to be his friend?"

Katie turned from the window and looked at her roommate. She folded up the letter that she held in her hands and said softly, "It's all I dare hope for."

Chapter 28

STEADY RAIN

Indian Summer lingered with its warm, sunny days and crisp, cool evenings. The leaves on the trees had turned into vibrant shades of orange, gold and red. Katie hoped the nice weather would continue through the weekend. Wayne was due to arrive that afternoon for his visit. Katie glanced at the clock on the dresser: 2:17. Her classes were over for the day and she could not concentrate on any schoolwork. The afternoon was dragging.

Sara breezed into the room and laid a pile of library books on her desk. "He's still not here?" she asked, eyeing Katie. "What time did he say his flight was getting in?"

Katie shrugged, "He didn't say." She got up from her chair, went to the window and then over to the door. The small dorm room did not allow much room to pace. "He was kind of vague about the details, but he can be that way. I guess he's taking a cab. He just told me not to worry, he'll be here between one and three."

"Okay. Did you make arrangements for him to stay in guest housing?"

"Yes," Katie's words were cut off by their phone ringing. Sara, standing the nearest to the receiver, answered it. Her eyes shone with excitement as she listened to the message from the front desk clerk. "Okay, thanks," she said into the receiver. Hanging up the handset, she turned to Katie and announced, "He's here."

Katie smiled nervously at her roommate. "Do I look okay?" she asked. She had on light blue Capri pants with a checked shirt and her hair hung loose.

"Perfect," Sara assured her. "I probably won't see much of you the rest of the day, but tonight I'll be waiting to hear about everything. Now, go on," she gently turned Katie toward the door. "He's come a long way to see you; don't keep him waiting any longer."

Katie hurried down the hall and skipped down the steps to the first floor landing. Taking a deep breath, she pushed open the door to the dormitory lobby and stepped through. There were a couple of students pulling mail from their boxes and an upperclassman was flirting with the curly, blond-haired desk clerk. Katie looked past them all and took a few steps toward the meeting area of the lobby.

Wayne stood with his back to her, facing the window. Katie stood quietly for a moment, studying him. She was glad she had put on her good Capri pants since apparently Wayne had dressed up. He was not wearing his usual blue jeans, but instead wore khaki colored pants and a long-sleeved denim shirt. He shoulders looked filled-out so Katie assumed he had gained back most of the weight he had lost.

"Wayne," she said as she moved farther into the room, stopping about three feet from him.

At the sound of her voice, Wayne swung around to face her. In his hands was a large bouquet of Black-eyed Susans. Tears sprang to Katie's eyes at the sight of the flowers. Her eyes traveled from the bouquet up to his face and hair. He looked good. The dark circles under his eyes were gone. His hair was, as usual, a little unruly, but she could tell that he had attempted to make it behave. She looked deeply into his brown eyes and saw the sparkle she had missed all these past months. Looking into his eyes, she realized he was studying her, too. He was drinking in the sight of Katie with her green eyes and long blond tresses that lay in waves about her shoulders.

Katie was the first to speak. "You look good," she complimented, "really good. Healthy and happy and," she searched for a word as she compared him now to the last time she had seen him looking thin and depressed, "and strong," she finished.

Wayne visibly relaxed at her welcome. "Katie, you always have such a way with words. If I look good, then you look marvelous!

Here," he stepped over to her and held out the bouquet, "these are for you. Black-eyed Susans."

Katie smiled and accepted the flowers. "I can see that. I love them. Thank you."

Wayne shifted his weight. "You remember, don't you? The flowers in Montana?"

Katie looked down at the flowers, then back into his brown eyes. "I remember." She smiled and said gently, "I'm surprised that you remember."

"I remember everything that concerns you, Katie. Like the fact that you are probably the only girl who would say she loves the wind and Minnesota icicles."

Katie's mouth opened in disbelief. "Did I tell you that? And if I did, you remember?"

He nodded. "That day you had the flat tire. I figured you had to be a rather special girl to love crazy stuff like that." He looked around the lobby and considered the other students in the area. "Is there some place we can go to talk? We have a lot to talk about. At least, I do. Is now an okay time for you?"

"Yes, it's perfect," Katie assured him. "I cleared my whole weekend for you. I've been so looking forward to your visit. Let's go outside. We can walk over to the pond behind the library."

Wayne followed Katie as she led the way out of the lobby doors and began to walk across campus, carrying the flowers. Wayne caught up to her and fell in step beside her. He did not want to start the conversation yet so he remained quiet. He wanted to wait to say anything important until he could face her, until he could look into her face and watch for her reactions. He felt he could read Katie's expressions like a book.

Katie began chatting about the college, telling him what each building was and how many students went there. When they rounded the library, Wayne saw a few other couples lounging beside the pond, but Katie led him over to a place on the other side, far enough away from the others to insure privacy. She sat down on the grass and laid the flowers next to her. Wayne lowered himself to the ground and sat cross-legged directly in front of her. Katie crossed her legs, too, and scooted forward so they were sitting only an arm's length away from each other.

"I want to hear about your trip," Katie said lightheartedly.

"Later," Wayne's tone was serious. "I have a lot of other things to say first. The way I feel right now, that just might take all weekend."

"I'm not going anywhere," Katie said, her heart beginning to flutter nervously.

Wayne drew on his courage and dove in. "First of all, I'm sorry. A long time ago, I made declarations to you that I would always be there for you, and I let you down big time when it really mattered. Then, when you tried to remind me of it, I pushed you away."

"I understood. I didn't like it, but I understood."

Wayne looked at her challengingly. "I hurt you, Katie. You were already hurting as badly as anyone possibly could be and I hurt you even more. Why can't you admit it?"

Katie nodded slowly. It was true, he had hurt her, but she wanted to make excuses for him. "I know that you did it out of desperation and self-preservation. I could see that. I tried to give you your space and honor your wishes."

"You did, Katie, you did. And you are partially right about my reasons, but I would rather cut off an arm than hurt you like that again. I should have been there for you, especially at first, during the week of the funeral. I should have taken my eyes off myself and looked out for you, and my parents, and my brothers," Wayne's voice faded away momentarily. "I need to say I'm sorry for all that. I need to ask you to forgive me." Tears pooled in his eyes as he waited for her answer.

Now Katie's heart was hammering in earnest to see Wayne, a strapping young man, humble himself before her like this. "I do forgive you," Katie said sincerely. "Friends forgive each other, Wayne, and I've always been your friend."

"Our friendship is a whole separate issue, Katie. One we *will* talk about, but I need to take care of one thing at a time. I need to be sure this one is completely settled."

"I forgive you," Katie told him again. "What can I say to convince you?"

Wayne studied Katie's face for a few moments. Feeling satisfied, he acknowledged her. "Thank you. This is a big issue with me. On the trip, with my Uncle Brad, I worked through a lot of things. I spent a lot of time in prayer and I know without a doubt, that God has forgiven me. When I got home, I made apologies to my family and to Diana, and Matt, too. Everyone has forgiven me, but your forgiveness has mattered the most. It's one more burden I can let go of now."

Wayne and Katie sat in silence for several minutes. Katie wanted to let Wayne continue to lead the conversation. She knew that he had an agenda so she waited quietly until he was ready to move on.

Wayne looked at the pond as he formulated his thoughts. Leaves were floating down from the surrounding trees and some landed on the surface of the water. A few gray clouds began to form in the sky so occasionally the sun was hidden and the couple would be cast in shadows. Wayne felt a lump in his throat, but knew it was now or never to speak his mind.

Taking a deep breath, he returned his eyes to hers, and began. "Katie, I can't be your friend anymore. I didn't come here so that things between us could be like they were before."

Katie felt her heart breaking as her eyes filled with tears. This was the last thing she had expected to hear from Wayne. "But your letter and the flowers… I thought…" Katie could not go on as she struggled not to let the tears come.

Wayne brought his knees up to his chest and, putting his arms around them, grabbed one of his wrists with the palm of his other hand. "Katie, I need you to listen to me. Please, don't say anything until I'm done. I need you to really hear what I'm about to say. Can you do this?"

Pressing her lips together, Katie nodded. She was beginning to feel sick to her stomach, but she would listen to him with all her heart. She could not believe he had come two thousand miles to say goodbye to her again.

"This is really hard for me, Katie. It might be the hardest thing I have ever done. I'm not sure how to get you to understand." Wayne took his eyes off her for a moment. It was too hard for him to concentrate when Katie had tears in her eyes. He just wanted to wipe them away. Pulling himself together, he returned his eyes to her face and started again. "I don't know when it started. I never meant for this to happen, but I guess that I've felt this way for a long time now. I mean, we were friends, right?"

Katie, beginning to feel perplexed, nodded her head.

"Katie, we started out as friends, but somewhere along the way, I fell in love with you." *There. I said it.* Wayne took a deep breath before he continued. "It's been a real struggle for me. I mean, you belonged to Steve. When I was on my trip, I came to terms with the fact that he doesn't have any claim on you anymore. That maybe, he would even welcome the thought that someday you would be with me. I think he would appreciate that I would take really good care of you." Wayne did not bother to blink away his tears. "I'm not saying this very well, Katie. When I said that I couldn't be friends with you, that I didn't come here so things could be like they were before, I meant that. It's because I love you." A tear ran down his cheek and dripped onto his leg. "I mean, really love you. I can't go back to *just* being your friend." He noticed tears were beginning to fall from Katie's eyes, too. "I don't mean to put pressure on you, but I *need* you, Katie Fremont. I have to ask, is there anyway that you think you could learn to love me, too?"

Katie was still holding her lips tightly closed. Tears were rolling slowly down her face, but she did not brush them away. She saw an occasional tear run down Wayne's face. She reached up and with one finger wiped a tear off his cheek, then said, "I never dreamed that you felt this way about me. I know that back in high school we were friends. Then, after the accident, I just wasn't sure any more. I thought you blamed me and if anything, only tolerated me."

"I can see how you would have thought that. I did blame you for a while, but I think partially why I pushed you away after Steve died was because I was already loving you; I just hadn't figured it out yet. I guess I felt guilty, but I didn't know why."

So many things were starting to make sense to Katie now. "Well, back then I did just want to be your friend, because I thought you didn't like me anymore. I thought your anger and hurt had pushed me away for good. After Steve died, it was hard. Really hard. We both know that. What made it even harder for me was losing you as well as him. When you walked away from me at the mall that night, it really hurt. I didn't want to lose your friendship. Wayne, you and I have been through so much together. You were there with me at the very beginning." Katie sniffed and put her hand on one of Wayne's. "But when you walked away from me in August, right before your trip, I began to realize that what I felt for you went beyond friendship. I was absolutely devastated. It hurt too much to just be a friend thing, but I never dreamed you would ever feel the same about me. I just kept hoping that someday I would have you in my life again as a friend." Katie cocked her head and tenderly smiled at him. "I guess what I'm trying to tell you is that, yes, I think I am already beginning to love you."

Wayne gripped her hand tightly. "You have much more courage than I do, but I guess I always knew that. Coming out here to Minnesota, I convinced myself that I had to have all or nothing. It sounds like you were willing to take as much or as little as I had to offer you." He smiled from ear to ear. "It sounds like you are going to take much, because that is what I'm offering." He hesitated a moment and then said, "Come on, can we go for a walk? I'm getting stiff sitting on the ground." Wayne rose to his feet, and reaching a hand down, gave Katie a pull. She picked up her flowers as she stood up. He kept her small hand in his as they aimlessly wandered away from the pond, away from the buildings and toward the road that led off campus and wound through a quiet, shady neighborhood. The clouds were getting darker and heavier, nearly blocking the sun out completely.

"Katie," Wayne continued their conversation, "I am sure a lot of people would tell me that I am completely crazy to talk to you like this less than a year since Steve died, but I'm going to let you be the judge of that. You've given me some hope and I'm going to run with it." He glanced down at her as they walked. "I want to share my life with you, Katie. I need you to be a part of my life, and I want to be a part of yours. I'm not talking about just as friends. Do you understand what I am saying?"

"I think so," Katie said softly, thinking about the way the most unexpected things were happening today. "I want to share your life, too." She squeezed his hand. "Like I said, I'm already falling in love with you."

Wayne's heart was soaring now, but he felt that he still needed to clarify a few things. "I'm not talking about a public engagement. It's way too soon for that. I'm thinking about a private understanding between the two of us. Before I came here, I talked with my folks and told them a little about how I feel. I think, at least for now, we shouldn't say anything more to our families or to Diane or anyone. When the time seems right, we can make some kind of announcement. I'm not naïve. I realize we will have a lot of things to work through."

Katie only nodded. She wanted to hear everything he had to say.

"I know that I am not at all like Steve was. We had a lot of fun and shared a lot, but we were really very different." He stopped walking and turned Katie around to face him. "I'm not a sweet talker or a gentleman like Steve was and I don't want to wonder if you are always comparing us. He and I were not just brothers, but great friends, and we loved each very much. I know that you loved him too, but I don't want to feel like I'm playing second fiddle to Steve. You and I can keep him as a part of us, because he was a very big part of both of our lives, and I believe he always will be, but I don't want him *between* us, do you understand?"

Katie nodded. "I loved Steve for who he was. Ours was a very sweet and innocent first love. I will never forget it or him and he'll always have a place in my heart. My relationship with him came about very quickly. You know that, you were there. I fell in love with Steve in a whirlwind. I think I'm falling in love with you in a steady rain."

Wayne grinned as a first raindrop hit him on the head. "I think God has a great sense of humor." He looked up at the clouds and another raindrop splattered onto his chin. "Katie," he lowered his eyes to hers, "I love the idea of us falling in love gradually. What started out as friendship is just blossoming and growing into love." More sprinkles of rain fell around them and Katie felt as if her heart was swelling with joy and hope.

"I need you, Katie," Wayne told her. "I think that having you to share my life will make me feel complete. I want us to walk side by side. For one thing, I can't wait to tell you about what I saw and did on my trip and I can't wait to take you with me on my next one." He turned her around so they could begin walking again.

"You know something?" Katie asked in a pensive tone. "I didn't realized this before, but Steve never told me he needed me."

Wayne squeezed her hand. "No comparisons, remember?"

The couple continued down the sidewalk, not seeming to care that rain was dripping on them through the tree branches that lined the street. "Where are we going?" Wayne asked Katie.

"I don't know," she shrugged. "I want to keep talking to you. We have seven months worth of things to talk about and I don't want to do it on campus where it's so hard to find a quiet corner. I came to college without my car, so we can't go too far."

"What are you talking about?" Wayne asked. "I have my car here. It's over in the lot behind your dorm."

Katie screwed up her face in a look of confusion. "Wayne Anderson, are you telling me that you drove out here from Washington? I thought you flew."

"This is the deal," Wayne turned her around yet again so they were heading back toward campus. "I took a gamble. I packed up all my stuff. I mean *all* my stuff." He looked seriously at Katie. "Not just clothes for a week, but everything. I decided that I would offer you my heart. If you told me to get lost, then I would just turn around; head back home and put everything away. However," he dragged out the word and smiled, "if you took my heart in your hand and agreed to share my life, then I decided I would stay here. I'll find a place to live, get a job somewhere and start school second semester. I'll be a year behind now, but I want to get back on track with my education major. You'll be finished in two years, Katie, and well, we'll see what happens." He stopped walking again and stood in front of her. He took both of her hands in his and looked deeply into her eyes. "I am never going to walk away from you again."

THE END

Printed in the United States
1175400006B/78-99